Shadows of Pendle

Edited by Barry McCann
and
David Saunderson

Printed in the United Kingdom

First Printing, 2018

ISBN 978-1-9164227-0-4

Dark Sheep Books
Flat 24
316 Green Lanes
Manor House
London, N4 1BX

For more offerings from the night side of the fold, see
www.darksheepbooks.co.uk

CONTENTS

Introduction

Known as "The Roof of Lancashire" Pendle Hill stands just 1,827 feet short of being a mountain. Nevertheless it casts a long shadow across the county's history thanks to certain events of 1612, the consequences of which are still felt today.

While many people have heard of The Pendle Witches few probably know the tragic story behind them, one of innocents unwittingly caught up in a climate of superstition, suspicion and ruthless political ambition.

The England of 1612 was charged with paranoia, much of it bred by King James I. He had written the book Demonology in 1597 which attributed the supernatural powers of witches to demonic possession, and was convinced witches were being used by political rivals to cast spells against him.

The Gunpowder Plot of 1605 reinforced James's oppression of non-conforming English Catholics, resulting in the Popish Recusants Act 1606 that required every citizen to take an Oath of Allegiance denying the Pope's authority over the king. Though conciliatory towards Catholics who took the Oath, he was harsher to those who did not and regarded them as idol worshipping witches.

James also commissioned of a new translation of the Bible partly influenced by his work on Demonology and confirming the divine right of kings to rule, published just a year before the unfolding of events at Pendle overseen by court appointed Magistrate Roger Nowell.

What better way for Nowell to please his masters in London than convictions using His Majesty's anti witchcraft laws. And providence delivered that opportunity when members of two feuding local families – the Device's and the Whittle's came up before him on a case of petty theft, which then turned into accusations of witchcraft between both clans.

As it turned out, both families were headed by two senile old women convinced they were witches, and members of their families also believed they had inherited their power and all too ready to confess. Though Nowell was slow to act on the initial accusations, a subsequent incident involving the apparent cursing of a pedlar by Alizon Device led to initial arrests and detention at Lancaster Castle. His pursuit became more enthusiastic as others came into the frame, thanks to news of a secret Good Friday gathering at the Device's home, Malkin Tower, reaching his ears.

Everyone reportedly present at the meeting found themselves swept up into Nowell's bag and delivered to Lancaster for the August assizes. And what followed could be described as a show trial in which the youngest of the Device family, nine year old Jenet, was unexpectedly produced as the key witness for the prosecution. The child sensationally identified and denounced each of the accused of being witches, including her own mother.

On August 20th 1612 Jenet became the only surviving member of the Device's as her mother and siblings were sent to the gallows. How exactly the child was honed into betraying her own kin remains a mystery, as does her whereabouts during the months between the detention of her remaining family and their trial. Undoubtedly, Roger

Nowell had the child taken care of, during which she was indoctrinated as a tool of his machination.

There is also a question mark over another accused of attending the Good Friday gathering, Alice Nutter, a property owning catholic who, it is believed, was in a land dispute with Nowell. If this was true, her arrest and execution would have been a convenient problem eliminator.

Speculations such as these are key to the myth making of the Pendle Witches. Like Jack the Ripper, their story is rooted in historical events shrouded with mystery, those gaps in knowledge filled by speculation which, over time, have become interwoven with fact. The real life Pendle Witches were no more pointy hatted crones of flying broomsticks than the Whitechapel murderer was a top hatted cloaked figure armed with a Gladstone bag. But don't we just love that myth.

Shadows of Pendle is a collection of newly commissioned stories and poetry, inspired by the legend of the Witches. They encompass the facts, the fancies and the myths in dramas ranging from the darkly psychological, paranormal, fantasy and horror.

Beginning with the actual true story as seen through the eyes of an adult Jenet Device, the tales range from speculation as to how the two family heads, Elizabeth Southern and Ann Whittle, became rivals; of how the fallout of their powers reached across space and time, touching the lives of others, and through to contemporary times with deadly consequences.

Along with the stories are interludes of poetry, foregrounding the dramas and tragedy borne out of this dark period of history, reminding us of the truth behind the tales. In short a collection with something for everyone.

The authors include established writers and those relatively new to the printed word, based not just in the United Kingdom but also the United States and Europe. And all are bewitched by one muse; the spectre of Pendle and its children, whether infernal or tragic. So beware, will you fall?

Jennet Device
by Gordon Aindow

Not much by way of affection:
hard words
followed by hard hands
more the order of things.
There may have been calling on spirits
and dogs I hadn't seen before
but there were always dogs around.
I'm not saying they talked
or did much of owt.

It's not right to be treated so hard
spoken to as though you're nothin'.
I'm not nothin'.
I'm Jennet.
My name's Jennet.
I'm summat.

The hat man - magistrate man -
wants summat.
I knows it.
Wants to hear of the cursing,
the spells
the witchifying.
I'll tell him.
Tell him of the spells, curses,
the appearance of beasts:
mainly dogs.

I'll show 'em
show 'em all I'm summat.
Not some small, beaten snot of a thing,
a nothin', only right for hard handlin'.
I'm summat.
I'll tell.
I'll show 'em.
I'm Jennet.
They'll not forget.

Shouted at me in the court she did
spittle-mad with rage she were.
Took my mother away they did
and listened to me
to me, Jennet.
I'm not nothin'.

They'll hang for it they say.
That's them done for
done and gone
and no more raging at me.
Try your spells, curses
and summoning beasts now
if you can.
I'm done with you.
I'm not nothin'.
I'm Jennet.

The Reaper's Wind
by Barry McCann

Where does a nightmare begin? It unfolds so ordinarily, so unforeseen. A seed is planted and slowly grows, sprouting outwards, releasing new seed, new growth, spreading like a wild fire. But harvest time is not always the happiest of tales, and ours were the unhappy one. And all my childish wile did nothing to rescue our story from ending in ruination. For instead of saviour, I became reaper's scythe.

There I stood in that very court chamber where, twenty two summers previously, I were placed upon table to turn evidence against kith and kin. Only this time, it were my turn in the dock.

Judge looked down on me, as Nowell had all those years ago. He said "Are you Jennet Device, daughter of the parish of Newchurch in Pendle?"

Now there's a name not answered to in a long time, not since childhood. I've been other names since, but that one now returned to claim me. So I looked at him.

"Aye," I said, "some of the time." He frowned at me, "What do you mean by that? Some of the time?" I remember smiling back at his grunty face and saying "I am many others."

"Others?"

"Aye, your honour. I am Demdike, 'lizabeth, James, Alizon. I am all of them."

Well, he didn't like that at all. Grumpily, he cleared his throat and loomed over me more. "I am well aware of your wretched family history and caution you to thank the good Lord's mercy that the law which sent your kin to the gallows is ... well ... a little more lenient these days."

He didn't understand. No one can understand. I am my kin, kith and kin. How can folk know, when even educated gentry like him don't know. And he's wrong about law sending kith and kin to hangman. It weren't that, it weren't Nowell, it weren't Scotch Jimmy. It were me.

I remember that first evening well, in the hovel of the home so laughingly called Malkin Tower. Nine year old, I were, and runt of the litter. Mam was too busy preparing libations to bother with me. My brother, James, was down in Newchurch seeking free ale as usual and Alizon, my sister, was also late in returning home. So it were left with Grandem to have me take to my bed, and it were same ritual every time.

She would say "Listen to that wind, Jennet. Listen carefully now for soon you shall hear the sound of hoofs trotting in distance of wind. It blow from Jinny Lane and the hoofs belong to the 'eadless 'orseman, out on his rounds. He seeks naughty childer who don't take to their cribs when told. So listen and beware, but don't fancy peeking. 'Cos if you peek, he'll know. And he'll come galloping for you. And you may hide in your crib, but he'll find you and take your 'ead. And he'll take it back to hang from his tree along with others he's taken. And there they all swing in the Reaper's wind. So listen for the hoofs, Jenet." Then she'd tap out time with her fist on top of my head. "And when clip clop turns clipity clop... clipity clop turns clipity, clipity clop, then be knowing that some

8

wretched infant peeked and will forfeit 'ead for its trouble."

Grandem loved filling my head with unholy tales such as this. So, eventually, I would give in and retire to my crib. Grandem then settled down in her chair by the fire, her eyelids resting closed and her soul soon elsewhere. But I was not asleep when Alizon burst through the door like a woman taken by a thousand devils. Her eyes were wide, even the bad one, and her countenance was that of panic. Grandem's eyes shot open and Mam stopped what she was doing, as Alizon spurted "God help me now!" Mam took her by the hands and bad her sit down while asking "What posseses you! What's happened?"

"I've done it now! Used my power and it went wrong. I didn't mean for it to happen." Mam handed my sister a bottle of one of her brews and had her take a mouth full to calm her tempered brow. She took a few breaths and then shared her tale.

"I was on way to Trowden to see if pickings to be had there. And Ball was with me, right by my side." Ball was Mam's familiar, you see. She said it took the form of a hound, but I could never see it. When Alizon went out that morning, Mam told her to take Ball for protection. Seemed this may have been a mistake.

"Then this peddler came walking from the other way and I could see he was carrying pins. So Ball whispered in my ear, saying "There you are, Alizon. Try asking him for some nice pins. You could treat warts with those, and other things." So I stepped before him and said "Afternoon, sir. Nice day." But he were angry and said "Never mind the day. Be out of my road, wench!" So I said "Don't be like that. I'm only after enquiring if you could spare this poor wench some pins, for I have none."

"Then he raised his hand in threat and bellowed "Pins, is it? Out of my way, I'll see less of thy mischief!" So I stepped out of his path and he walked on. But Ball whispered in my ear, saying "You're not going to stand for that, are you? Go on, set me on him. That's what I was given to your mam for. Just give the word, Alizon!" So I summoned up all my power and pointed at the stranger, shouting "Ball! That peddler! Go, fetch!" And he did. He brought him down, and the man was seized, his face twisted."

"Is he dead?" Mam croaked. "Ney, he lives, but his body's cursed. He managed to get up and make an inn nearby. I followed and begged his forgiveness. But devil has his voice now."

"Where there others there?"

"Aye, there were folk attending to him." Mam's concern turned into anger. "Foolish child! I taught thee to keep thy gift cloaked! Now they know!" Alizon nodded tearfully "What will come of this?"

Well, folk all know what came of it. Both Alizon and Grandem were soon up before Magistrate Nowell and readily confessed to spell making. They were sent to Lancaster for their trouble, to await assizes. And then, Mam and James had that gathering in Malkin Tower. There were a fair few in attendance. Jane Bulcock came along with her son, John, who entertained us with jests that my child mind couldn't understand.

"How do you confuse a Puritan? Put him in a barrel and tell him to make water in the corner." He said. "D'ye ken why it takes three puritans to shoe horse? One to work bellow, other to forge shoe and third to pray for the Almighty's blessing in this arduous task." And they all laughed.

Then, Alice Nutter arrived. Why someone so well to do should be present among likes of us was beyond my reason. But it was that presence that was to condemn her and, very likely, the others. There were whispers Nowell were in dispute with Alice over the boundary of their adjoining lands. Now, if one accuses another of witchery, and that accusation secures conviction, then everything belonging to accused became that of accuser. Such a convenient arrangement that must have presented our magistrate. Not only does he please Scotch Jimmy by bagging witches, but rids himself of an irritation of his own.

Thus, news of the gathering reached his ears and the three of us were summoned to Read Hall. Mam and James were accused of holding a black mass and plotting to rescue our kin by blowing up Lancaster Castle. Soon, they were packed off there to join them and there was no one to look after this fatherless sprite. So Magistrate took me in, promising I would be cared for and educated. I became resident at Read Hall, under the wing of its kindly housekeeper who kept me washed and generously fed. I had a nice soft bed and clean clothes, but knew little of the price that would come with these comforts.

In the evenings after supper, Magistrate would send for me and bid I sat by the crackling fire with him. He would chat, often about my kin and their doings. I would tell him things, and he would steer me into what he said were the truths of these things. I were so eager to please, that I saw what he wanted me to see, and he would then tell me what I clever girl I am. He was like the Father I never had, you see.

Then one night he told me I would have to testify at assizes and, if I spoke with honesty, my family would no longer be imprisoned. So he schooled me in the truth to be told. But this were his truth, not the real tale. He moulded me like a clay doll and my compliance spared the others any further languish in gaol, as he promised. What he didn"t admit is that it spared them for hangman. What a young fool I'd been, this very maiden putting noose around their necks. Me, obliging Nowell as his marionette.

And that be the truth of it, Magistrate Nowell's little bandling. Oh, yes, he whistled and to his tune I danced all right! Queer turn of events, then, that thirty year on I'm in gaol for witchery and it were a child who pointed finger at me. A boy, little older than I when placed upon table as denouncer of my kin. How damningly poetic!

Thus, when my accuser were brought forward and presented, I saw myself. Now I am Edward Robinson, a precocious child who dances to bidding of a schemer. His father approached me in Newchurch, threatening to have the brat accuse me of witchcraft unless I gave him money, and other favour. So I spat in his eye and told him to go favour with himself. If only I had Ball, as my sister had. I'd have unchained him onto that bastard!

For yes, I am a witch. A truth my blackmailer's deceit touched upon and the fool did not even know it. But I was not about to oblige with any ready confession as Alizon had done. I give them nothing, even if that is all it will bring me.

Still, Judge was right that law's changed since my kin met hangman, and I fancy cheating his noose. Don't know about lenient, mind. Gaoler reckons I'll do stocks, or longer spell in his care with forfeit to pay. Not that I reckon much to his care, I've seen look on his leering face. Still, managed to grab lock of his hair when he put his grubby paw on me the other day. Just need a candle and dance to my song, he will.

But whose song am I dancing to? Why did I take up craft after what it did for them? After what I did to them? I fancy Grandem steered me into it, even from her grave. And getting caught is revenge for the words I gave away at Assizes. Wheel's turned and I'm in spot they were.

But that be not enough for Grandem. Fancy she'll send horseman to do hangman's job. He'll take my head, and take it to his tree. And there, in reaper's wind, it'll swing … and swing … and swing.

Bad Blood by Ruby Red

For Elizabeth Southern the Hill had always been forbidden fruit. In childhood her mother repeatedly forbad she ever ascended it as "no good" awaited up there. A single path led up to the forbidding peak, one few dared to tread outside daylight. Folk spoke of it being more ancient than the Roman Roads that cut across the county. In fact, it was said even the legions themselves dared not traverse it.

However there was one evening when, following a few libations, her mother's loosened tongue admitted to once giving into curiosity and daring that pathway. But the journey was cut short when a large boulder came rolling down from nowhere, forcing her to jump out the way. It was clear she was not welcome and, whatever secrets lay uphill, it resolved to keep them to itself.

But Elizabeth had taken to gazing up at that same peak of late, for sure that it was staring back down at her. Her instincts began to hear it calling and up there the solution to her rivalry with Ann Whittle lay waiting to be found.

Up until a few months previously Elizabeth and Ann were friends, and had been since childhood. Such a bond is hard to break, but it took a young man new to the area to do so. He arrived in Pendle to work on one of the farms, and his strikingly handsome features quickly attracted the lustful gaze of local maidens.

Fancying themselves as suitors, both Elizabeth and Ann had courted him, neither aware each other had submitted to his advancements. However, upon finding out, they took against one other and competitively flirted with the man in the hope of being chosen for his bride. As the rivalry turned fiercer, it became increasingly bitter. They say blood runs deep, but bad blood runs the deepest.

While her mother had become a God fearing woman over the years, Elizabeth's grandmother was versed in the old ways and taught them to her as a young girl. Mainly charms and incantations for protection, but there were other spells that professed to remove obstacles. The problem was, while Elizabeth knew the basics of casting hex, she did not have the power. That was a secret her gran had passed onto her mother, whose subsequent change to a devout Christian meant she would never impart it.

It took the relentless determination to get rid of Ann Whittle for Elizabeth to finally connect her mother's scare stories about the hill with the secret she refused to speak of. It seemed there was where the answer lay.

Choosing an evening of full moon, Elizabeth added something extra to her mother's broth, ensuring she would be in deep slumber before the witching hour. Wrapping herself in a cloak, she lit a torch from the burning embers of the open fire and stepped outside into the coldness of night. She contemplated the way before her with apprehension, and then the journey into a new unknown began.

After a while, she paused and rested on a boulder while glancing back down at the village, and then back up. It was taking longer than anticipated, but remained resolved to find what she sought. There was no going back now.

As the trail became steeper, a shape emerged from the darkness ahead. The sound of heavy snorting, followed by the slow pace of a beast on gravel coupled with glaring, yellow lantern eyes suggested something fearful.

Stopping in her tracks, Elizabeth was confronted by a black hound with a long pointed snout and a tail that remained still. It stood ground and, much to her surprise, spoke.

"Greetings, Elizabeth Southern. Which perplexes you more? My speaking, or knowing thy name?" Its mouth moved more like that of a man than beast.

"Do all dogs up here spake as you?"

"A dog is what you see. I take many forms."

"If thy know my name, then know my business," she bravely replied.

"Aye, thy purpose is known. Thou afflicted with an itch that only Scratch will out."

"Will take more than scratch to remedy Ann Whittle."

"Then I bequeath to you the means by which to deal with her thyself. And others who would cross thee."

"And by what payment?"

"No payment, Elizabeth. I be your guide and familiar, as I was to your grandmother. Say you accept?"

"I shall not depart empty handed."

"Then we are in accord."

With that, the creature stepped forward and kissed each of her feet, then her knees. It stood on hind legs to kiss her abdomen, before its body elongated and stretched upwards to kiss her breasts. Once fully erect, its mouth pressed upon hers with tongue protruding. Once the ritual was complete, the creature withdrew and its yellow eyes looked straight into those of Elizabeth. "You call me Tibb."

With her mother still safely asleep by the time she returned home, Elizabeth set to work without haste. From a box hidden under her bed, she produced a small scroll of parchment and a quill before uncorking a bottle of lamb's blood to serve as ink. Carefully, she inscribed the parchment with runic symbols taught by her gran, weaving a curse that promised death to the one in possession of it within three days. Once blessed in the stream of moonlight, she then had to ensure it found itself about Ann Whittle's person before the deadline was up.

An opportunity arose just the following morning when Elizabeth spotted Ann entering the church with basket hanging waist high from her folded arm, doubtless to fill with pickings from the Harvest Festival. A ruse occurred and she waited patiently for Ann to emerge, her basket now rich with apples. Conspiring to close in, Elizabeth calculated her steps so they would pass each other within the gateway. As their confronting faces met, Ann obliged with the opening shot.

"Praying forgiveness for whoring with my man, Jezebel?" Elizabeth loomed up to her, hissing "Your man? You serve as nowt but Sodom!" She then stood back as Ann stormed off, unaware of the rolled parchment slipped under the cloth that lined her basket.

Three dawns came and went, and the due time had passed. Yet, Elizabeth saw Ann in the village and about her business, evidently unharmed. Retreating back to Malkin Tower, Elizabeth stared into the flame of a candle wondering why the spell had not come to pass, and then realised one possibility. If Ann had handed the basket to somebody else, the parchment still within it, then the curse would pass to them. There had been no news of any death in the area as yet, but the parchment could have travelled far in just a couple of days. The strategy had misfired and she should have cast a spell aimed at Ann specifically. With eyes still fixed on the candle an idea presented itself and Elizabeth grinned. There was just one other ingredient that needed to be obtained.

Market day came to Barley, a time when traders and peddlers gathered with their wares. Knowing Ann would turn up looking to haggle for bargains, Elizabeth arrived early with a plan already connived and involving the stall that sold bonnets.

Sure enough, Ann Whittle turned up with her basket and meandered from trader to trader, closely inspecting the goods on offer. Elizabeth positioned herself ready behind the bonnet stall until Ann was stood in front eyeing up the stock. Her gaze turned to one of surprise as Elizabeth emerged into view.

"Hello, Ann." She said through the veneer of a warm smile. Ann shrugged and replied "How goes the day?" The formality of her tone made her hostility still quite clear.

Elizabeth stepped closer to her. "Sister, should we not quarrel over a man? It is he who will have to choose, thus let him decide. And if you he pleases, so mote it be. What say you, friend?"

Anne glanced down in thought for a few moments, before looking back up and slowly smiling. "Aye, there be wisdom in your words. And should thee be the one he favour, then so be it."

They both let out a short laugh of relief, and then Elizabeth turned to one of the bonnets hanging on display and picked it up. "I ponder this for my poor cold head, but with no looking glass know not how it will look." She held it up to Ann. "Try it on for me?"

Ann gave a smiling shrug and Elizabeth placed the bonnet on her head, tidying her hair under it. "Looks fair upon thee," she declared.

"Will look fairer on thee, I fancy," Ann replied.

"I shall make it mine." Elizabeth carefully removed the bonnet, ensuring at least a lock or two of Ann's hair came with it. Making the purchase, she folded the bonnet and carefully stowed it inside her smock. After engaging Ann in further polite niceties for a few moments more, she took leave and departed back to Malkin Tower, smirking with mischievous intent.

Ensuring she was alone, Elizabeth lovingly crafted a wax effigy. Smugly and with absolute conviction, she attached Ann's hairs to the waxen texture with some of her sacred pins, and then arranged the others on her smock for the ceremony later. Upon finishing, she whispered about its head and shrouded it in a black sack cloth.

After supper, she sneaked out of her home and into the darkness, clutching and clinging to the doll as if her life depended on it. Approaching the undergrowth she hid the doll about her person, constantly checking no one was following. Deep into Pendle Forest she tread, searching for a previously chosen tree.

Arriving at her destination, Elizabeth leaned against its trunk and sighed with relief. Chanting, she withdrew the doll from her undergarments, nodding as to confirm the final part of the plan.

Focused and eyes staring, she uncloaked the doll, and pinned it to the bark in an orchestrated manner. Employing sexual magick and wilful intent, she set about sealing the fatal and untimely death of Ann Whittle.

She lifted her skirt and unveiled her crotch, placing one hand on it and stroking gently. The other hand slowly removed the last remaining pin from her smock and, pausing in a moment of arousal, she stated purpose with hand poised for the final push into the doll. Her tongue rolled along moistened lips, enjoying a vision of sadistic pleasure and fatality fitting for her victim.

The following morning Elizabeth awoke feeling content and decided to wander into the village, hoping to learn of any news regarding Ann Whittle. She displayed a happy countenance amongst the villagers until spying Ann very much alive and chatting with friends. Cursing, Elizabeth withdrew and hurried home, confused and angry as to why

Ann remained unharmed after a second attempt. She resolved to return the Hill at night fall and summon the Familiar.

With midnight closing, the moon and stars hidden behind cloud, Elizabeth guided her way with a flaming torch until reaching the part of the hill where she first encountered the beast. Forcefully, she planted the torch into the ground and cast circle, invoking the four quarters. She summoned Tibb by name, angrily commanding his presence. Soon, the sound of his paws thudded on the firm terrain.

"What be thy want?" He enquired.

"You knew my purpose last we met?"

"A time before I became familiar to thee, Mistress Elizabeth. Now you must instruct in words, I cannot act otherwise."

Elizabeth folded her arms and huffed. "Twice I have tried to hex Ann Whittle, and twice spell has failed. The magic thy granted serves me not."

"Have you asked yourself why? You look, but you don't see. The answer brazens before your eyes, plainly within their sight."

"You speak in riddles!"

"I point the way you fail to recognise." His snout indicated eastward. "Return to Newchurch this very hour. That you seek awaits there." With that, he turned and vanished into the night.

Perplexed, Elizabeth closed circle and picked up the slowly dying torch, making her way back along the trail before finding the path to Newchurch. With more solid ground beneath her feet, she walked briskly to dispel the increasing cold of the night air. Soon, the stile that heralded entrance into the village came into view, or at least its shape silhouetted by the moonlight that now shone from behind. But there was something different about it and, as she got closer, the flame from her torch revealed the figure of Ann Whittle leaning against the stone structure.

"How goes the evening, friend Elizabeth?"

"I've enjoyed warmer. What brings thee here on this night?"

"Awaiting your return, was advised to find thee here."

"By who? I told no living soul of my purpose."

Ann produced a small sack and from it extracted the wax effigy Elizabeth thought safe back in Pendle Forest. Placing it on the stile, she mused "Is this such business?" She then pulled out and waved the parchment with the runic curse. "Or this?"

Throwing the sack down, Ann opened her shawl to reveal naked breasts upon which rested a pentacle, hung from her neck and glistening brightly in the seductive moonlight.

"I also have Familiar." Her nemesis confirmed.

Before either could speak further, a howl cried from the distance of the hill. They turned and looked up towards the hilltop, straining to make out the dark shape in the distant dead of night.

The creature they both knew as Familiar looked down at them with eyes seeing further than any mortal could, and smiled like a man. Silently it changed shape to gain height and howled once more. Elizabeth and Ann stared back at each other, eyes blackened and locked in confrontation. Now learned of their true standing, the women were positioned and the game unleashed.

Pins
by Gordon Aindow

Why would you talk to someone like that, all hard-edged and cussed? I wasn't doing anything to him, I wasn't trying to rob him or nothing. I just asked, I did, just asked. Well you have to; what else can you do? So I did. I asked him for some pins, that's all, not the cups or plates or the nice stuff, and he did have nice stuff. But no, I didn't trouble him about any of that, just the pins. You have to when mother sends you out; she expects. More than that, she demands: you had better come back with something worth having or by hell you'll know about it! Old she might be, but she'll let you have it alright, and no supper or breakfast. So bringing something back is necessary. It's like the law.

I was just waiting, waiting by the road and watching the colours, feeling the day, feeling it change. Spring, you see, waking up; life coming back into the land. It's been resting and now you can feel it, if you just wait. Close your eyes…feel it. Different, eh? Yes, coming to…waking up. I was watching the stream babbling and dabbling, and the little dipper, he's at it, busy as me he is, in and out of those rocks. Better come home with something, he had. Me and the dipper, we're a pair. Always grafting. At it, we are, always at it. Smiling to myself, I'm sure I was, smiling with the love of spring in me and the toiling dipper, when he says I ain't got nothing for ye. Nothin for ye. And I come awake then out of a reverie and I see him: hard-faced man, closed his heart to me and the day and the life springing forth, and

I say, I ain't asked you. And he says no, but you will and I'm just telling you before you do, I ain't got nothing. Well that made it worse; that set my mind to it. If he had just shown some cheer for the day, had some kindness about him, I might've let it be, waited for the next one, but that did it. I said I'll have some pins off you today. He said you won't. I said I'll have some pins and I'll give you a blessing on your day and your labour. He wasn't having it. Walked on head down, chunnering to himself about gypsies and the like. I wouldn't mind but him no more than a tinker himself, walking to and fro from here to Yorkshire, round the farms and villages. What gives him the right, eh? All airs and graces and stuck up. I'll not have it. So I keep at him about the pins. We need them for our work: spells, curses. We need the pins for all of that and I'll av em.

I walk with him a while, keeping step, talking about the day and the beauty all around and how we've been lucky with this fine weather and how that must help in his line of work. He doesn't talk, just grunts a bit and keeps silent the rest of the time. I try and keep it nice and pay him many compliments, such as he's a goodly man, and I wager he has a fine family what loves him and cherishes his hard labour and the many miles he must trudge across the land. I am as sweet as the babbling stream water; I thinks to myself people like sweetness more than vinegar, so sweetness I'll be. Still nothing from him, no mellowing of countenance or manner. I must av those pins at least. A half-dozen would do and he'd be rid of me; gone I'd be and he could go on unhindered and me on with the reverie of the brook and dale and curlew call. I'll need something from him though. It's not as if our Jennet is up to much, wafting about the place as though she's mistress and her nowt but a girl. I don't know where she gets her airs from. It's not as if you can beat them out of her – mother's tried that but still the same she is, wan-faced and uppity. No, our Jennet won't have anything, not begged, scrounged or stole. No, me again. It will be down to me again. The brother won't have done much either. Oh, he'll have been out trying to hawk mother's cure-alls and comforters and he may have threatened a few farmers with curses and spells but he'll not have got much. Never does. He's favourite, so it's alright for him, he won't draw more than a sigh from the olduns, whereas me, different that is: if I come home with nothin it's all slaps and curses and 'useless Alison'.

I'm still walking abreast with the traveller and I haven't called him a tinker or any manner of names he might take umbrage at. I have been sweet and mild. He starts in on me: he has had enough of me, he says. Get ye gone and he'll report me and av me locked up. So I ask him what's up with him and why is he acting so angry and mean? I tell him I can get him a panacea that will take away his choleric mood and make him as sweet as a lark. I could too, give him one of mother's cure-alls. That would lift him high as the clouds. I say it wouldn't cost him much either and that I'd offer a blessing for free. He says away with ye, I'm not having any of it, and that there's nothing wrong with him that a warm fire, some fine ale and being rid of me wouldn't cure. Be off with ye, he says, or I'll av the magistrate on ye. I've had enough of him by then and I'm tired of his meanness and threats. I'm wearied of him dragging the day down and draining the light from it and of flattening out the spring in my step. So I stop, and start to walk back toward home. I'll spend some more time at the stream and try and get back the goodness of the day; I'll sit awhile and be open to all the hidden wafts in the air and the secret languages of creatures: the small beasts of earth and air. I'll soak that all in, I'll be right again. I'll be ready for the tirade at home then, I'll be protected. Who knows, I might meet another traveller and he may have some kindness about him or won't want to be rid of me. Either way I could still get something, enough to satisfy the old uns.

But he's still talking, tinker man. Saying how a man should be able to walk unimpeded, not be harassed by the likes of you...your lot...no better than...should be put away. On and on he goes and at first I'm not listening until I can't not listen, he goes on that much and that loud. So I've had enough. Quashed at home and now here in my world. I've put up with him and I tells him stop now! He goes on; he's worked up, he is, with spittle about his chops and hands dancing about. I warn you, I say. I've had enough of your hard words. Stop now or you won't be getting no blessing, you'll be getting cursed! Yet on he goes, his mouth working up a lather and the oaths flying.

You'll be getting cursed and you won't like it!

Babbling, he is, and I can't make out what he's saying through his fury, so curse him I do. Look straight at him and curse him so he'll stop. That brings him up, puts a chock on his mouth and his breathing goes funny. So does his walk, a limp and drag to his leg. Well that might teach him something. If your meanness takes all the warmth and giving from the day, takes all and shares not, then the day will want something back, it'll happen want to take something from you. Wobble on home, he will. He'll happen be alright later but maybe wiser for it.

Stood the Waited
by Darren Melia

Stood with eyes staring
At farms down below
Staring at a crossroads
Between farms where life does grow
Where mother left us last time
And where mother's low cry came
Before they took her from us
And tied her arms again.

Searched for, found and gotten
Taken to her last
Her words ignored, forgotten
Never a spell was cast
Tears of steam still running
O'er cheeks of flaming red
And burnt before the masses
That had always had her dead.

Now stood with my eyes staring
At farms down below
Staring at a crossroads
Where haters' children grow
I raise a dearest heart
In a grip that won't let go
And speak the words that were never
But now I make them sow.

I cast her spell upon you
And listen for your breath
I wait to hear it stopping
I wait to feel your death

The Intruders
by Jason D. Brawn

"Do you hear something?" whispered Shauna in my ear, instantly interrupting a dream about wandering in the darkened woods on my own. I was following the trail of a winding creek. The dream suggested tranquillity, but waking up to my partner's demanding enquiry, could have soon turned it into my worst nightmare.

Moonlight shone through the closed curtains of our bedroom and Shauna looked terrified. Terrified of what was outside, as well as of what was yet to come. Since we arrived in West Close Farm she had experienced nothing but unsettlement from the locals of a nearby village called Higham. They all just stared at her silently, as if she weren't welcome. I never endured that kind of ordeal, and this trip was much-needed. We had to get away from the hectic surroundings of London. Besides, our eleven-year-old relationship was also in jeopardy, and this trip was our last resort to try to make it work. Yes, the villagers didn't welcome us holding hands when walking side-by-side, although that was the norm back in cosmopolitan and liberal London.

The heating should have been on, and my face felt the cold air. I was wrapped with a thick duvet and didn't want to get out of bed. I hoped it was a figment of her imagination. As the minutes passed, I waited to hear for any unpleasant sound, as it could have been a stag or a fox. Then I began to feel Shauna's rocking movements next to me. Sitting upright, she was too scared to leave the bed, but I could sense her urgent plea for me to see what was outside.

"What did you hear?" I wanted to know, almost raising my voice.

"Voices outside, chanting 'Get her!'" she hissed. I sensed she wanted me to speak quietly in case they were trying to overhear what was being discussed.

All right, I dared myself to check outside.

Once my bare feet touched the floorboards, I needed my slippers to resist the sudden cold underfoot. Still, I heard nothing suspicious, unless you count the whistling wind blowing heavily outside. Shauna remained in the toasty bed, waiting for my return.

I guess that I've always been her hero, I pondered, gazing at my useless girlfriend. Being three years older than me, she had experienced more than I had in life.

For the first time, I, too, felt vulnerable. *What if she were right?*

I moved swiftly towards the window.

"Do you hear it?" she hissed for my attention, hoping I would agree.

I heard nothing but the brief silence in the room.

"Hear what?" I enquired.

Shauna remained with her legs crouched on the bed, glaring at the window, hearing something for a few moments before her response was, "Whispers."

Again, I heard nothing but her frightened voice.

"Various voices and whispers."

When I turned to Shauna, her countenance was paralysed with fear. Her eyes widened and her lips quavered, desperate to utter more.

Daring myself, I rushed to the window and ripped open the curtains, seeing absolutely nothing but the night. Then Shauna said:

"They've stopped."

"Right, I'm gonna check outside," I declared, using my bravado to reassure her that there was nothing to worry about.

"Don't go!" she begged, burying herself with the covers by pulling them over her chest.

"You woke me up during my sleep - certainly there must be something outside!" I fumed at her, causing her to sob silently. "Now, I must confront what is out there," I continued, watching more fright fill her expression at my suggestion.

"Please, come back to bed," she insisted. "I don't want to be left alone."

"I won't be long," I promised, slipping on a pair of skinny tailored slacks, and lacing on a pair of Converses before zipping up my leather flight jacket to resist the cold air outside.

"Can't you wait 'til the morning?" she asked.

"No, because I know that tomorrow night, you will wake me up with the same old complaint," I predicted, grabbing a small torch from the dresser.

The moment I left the room, I heard the lock click on the bedroom door. She was already out of the bed, locking herself in the room until I returned.

The upstairs passageway was pitch black, except for the silhouettes of vases and a telephone chair by the stairs. I descended the stairs, soon landing on the ground floor passage. Now there was a little light, coming through the glazed window of the front door facing me.

When my hand touched the handle, it was mighty cold, like I was already outside. *Or was I?* I quickly turned with that dreaded thought. *Only my imagination.* I returned my gaze to the door, peering hard to see in the dark. *One, two, three!* I yanked the handle down, savagely hurling the door wide open and seeing - the branches of distant trees. They were swaying to and fro beneath the silver moon that was hanging far above in the night sky. The only noise I continued to hear was the intrusive wind that encircled the farmhouse.

So far, there was nothing spooky going on, but I felt the urge to continue checking the perimeter of the property.

While making tender footfalls, my Converses kept crunching foot on the gravel of the driveway. The light from my torch illuminated my path, picking up pebbles, trees, bushes and shrubs. I knew that I was rather far away from the main house, treading on the neatly trimmed lawn, but I had to be a hundred per cent certain that there was nothing nefarious going on. Never had I seen Shauna so scared and unsettled, not since we left London for our break.

Yesterday afternoon, there was an extraordinary episode Shauna told me about an elderly woman who made a claw sign on her face, intoning, "Devil lover," before telling her that the property was once owned by Anne Whittle and her daughter, Anne Redferne. This prompted my partner to do an online search for those names. She learned that Anne Whittle and her daughter were, in fact, convicted as witches, and later executed in the autumn of 1612, in connection with the Pendle Witches.

I supposed that every village had its own beliefs, but like Cornwall, the folks here did not like Londoners. Never mind that we came here as tourists to help boost the region's uncertain economy since Brexit! Then, Shauna did more research about the farmhouse. The last occupier vanished without a trace, prompting widespread media attention. Her body was found later. She had drowned in a nearby pool, but her face was badly battered and prick marks were embedded all over her arms and body in a sadistic style of torture.

Shauna was determined to leave immediately, but I convinced her to stay. I promised her that if anything odd occurred, I would deal with it. So here I was, awakened from my beauty sleep to fulfil my promise and ensure my girlfriend's safety.

Using the torchlight as my only source of guidance proved to be helpful but I soon developed an uncanny sense that I had walked far enough. The farmhouse was nowhere to be seen and there I was, all alone, in the windswept moorland.

It was time, I thought to myself, now retracing my steps back to the farmhouse. My shoes kicked the tall grass and bracken as I hurried back to the abode. The icy wind grew mightier, blowing me off balance and almost dropping me to the ground. I kept going and going, barely capturing a distant view of my place of residence. Jogging towards the house... I was getting nearer... and closer, but also very much out of breath and very tired.

I paused before the door and wished Shauna weren't such a fretful person. Then I noticed the door was slightly ajar.

I could have sworn I closed the door to protect Shauna in my absence.

My hand shoved the door, hearing it slam against the side furniture. I stormed in and raced up to the second floor bedroom. The door was already wide open and when I switched the light on, Shauna wasn't there! Messy bedcovers, a broken chair and perfume bottles that were knocked aside indicated an aggressive struggle.

"Shauna!" My voice broke into a hoarse cry. I was secretly hoping she was hiding. Then I stupidly checked the fitted wardrobes, in case she were there. But she was nowhere to be seen. "Shauna!" I screamed my heart beating rapidly and dreading the worst.

Immediately, I checked every room in the house, including the stone staircase in the kitchen. Not a trace. Strange that I saw and heard no intruder when I was outside. Stranger still that there was no car outside, nor did I hear an engine motoring about. This event was well beyond strange. It was as if Shauna simply vanished from the face of the Earth, much like the last unfortunate occupier of the farmhouse.

Then I halted at my thought!

I bolted out of the farmhouse, but noticed nothing. No tire tracks on the gravel drive and no sign of a forced entry. The front door was checked and it wasn't smashed in. As for the bedroom, the struggle could have easily been mistaken for the bedroom being rather unkempt.

I had one final resort.

"Police, I would like to report a missing person, please." I was rather polite when announcing my complaint.

"When did this happen?" queried the telephonist in a helpful and professional manner.

"Just now," was my honest answer. "I believe that she was kidnapped."

"Kidnapped?" the telephonist's inflection suggested she wanted to know more.

"Yes, she woke me up in the middle of night, mentioning something about some intruders. I went outside to have a look and when I returned she was gone," I explained.

"Where are you?"

"West Close Farm," I answered.

A long and thoughtful pause followed. I knew at once something wasn't right with the telephonist.

"We'll send someone straight away," came the hesitant reply.

"Thank you," I said, putting the phone back on its cradle.

Now, I was getting worried. Not only because the police might surmise that this event could be in related to the former tenant, but also that I could be next in line.

"Damn it!" I yelled, while calling myself a fool for not staying with Shauna. No instead I was venturing outside and acting brave.

* * *

The police arrived in no time and took fingerprints off the front door, bedroom door and every door of the house. I retold them my story, over and over again. They even checked outside the farmhouse, but saw no sign of any intrusion. The only footprints came from the soles of my Converses.

I should have left the farmhouse at once, but I was still there the next day. A patrol car was parked outside the farmhouse, guarding the property, in case they came back. I was slowly developing an uneasy feeling that they did not believe my story.

Later I went to the village of Barley, situated close to Pendle Hill, and noticed the residents glaring at me when catching sight of my appearance. As if I was infamous, not famous. Their expressions reflected their hate. The moment I visited The Pendle Inn for lunch, all their eyes landed on me, quiet and sullen. Afraid to eat there, in case my food was contaminated with saliva or rodent droppings, I stormed out of the pub and got back inside my car. Whilst I was turning on the ignition, the locals surrounded my car, and glared at me with their glowering eyes. They were ready to attack, judging by the looks on their faces, but a squad car was still across the road, ostensibly guarding me.

I drove off, heading back to the farmhouse, where I packed my belongings and Shauna's too. I knew that the authorities would be lax in their investigation and I didn't feel protected now, despite the police car parked outside. I could only wonder how long I would get their protection?

The moment I left the farmhouse, the police car was nowhere to be seen. I loaded our stuff into the boot of my car before locking the front door and dropping the keys through the letterbox. I promised I'd do that to the letting agent before renting this property.

The next time I switched on the ignition, the engine kept choking, and I knew the car was dead. My immediate thought was, *they did something to the engine.*

I called for an Uber taxi and was told that one would be at my location in fifteen minutes.

Waiting five minutes felt like half an hour. Waiting ten minutes was more like an hour and, after fifteen minutes, the glum impression that the taxi would never arrive crossed my mind.

Then a white car crept towards me, heading along the gravel driveway.

I rushed towards it and the driver's window slid down.

"Taxi?"

"Yes, love," replied the driver, a middle-aged man in his late fifties.

"Thank you so much," I desperately replied, eagerly showing my gratitude and appreciation for his long-awaited arrival.

I climbed inside the back before slamming the door. I didn't even bother to bring my belongings with me, being practically dying to leave this strange district.

"Lancaster railway station, please?"

The driver sped off. I refused to relax, not until I was on a train to London. I stared at the farmhouse, feeling very glad to see the last of it. I didn't even care much about the meter, as most punters do.

The car was being driven at a quick speed down various country roads. It seemed like the driver knew where he was going as the Sat Nav was off. But soon, my intuition told me to turn around, just in case I was followed. I did and noticed a car. It became further apparent when ten minutes later, the same car was on the taxi's rear.

"How far is it to the station?" I enquired.

"Taking the shortcut," he replied.

It didn't feel like any shortcut, as it was now fifteen minutes.

Another fifteen minutes later, he was still driving and there were now two cars following us. That didn't bother the driver, but it sure as hell concerned me. Then he made a swift turn at a slip road.

Now, it was clear that he was up to something.

"Why aren't you taking me to the station?"

He ignored me and his driving slowed down, taking us to a dirt road, surrounded by dense trees. More cars were tailing us.

"Where are we going?" I screamed at him, now panic-stricken and sensing imminent death.

He continued ignoring me, but I thought of a plan. A solution! The moment he stops, I will use my long nails and scratch out his eyes and claw his face, before running like hell into the woodlands.

The taxi slowed to a halt. He applied the brakes. The engine died.

Now!

But it was no use. People from all walks of life surrounded the taxi, staring at me, continuously chanting, "Get her!"

The driver opened his door, climbed out and slammed it shut before opening mine. I should have attacked him, but I was hopelessly crippled with fear. The locals pulled me out of the car, and I finally found the strength to constantly scream and kick wildly. There must have been over thirty or forty of them. I was summarily dragged and carried away, passing angry faces yelling "Witch!" I recognised some of them, including a duty officer from last night.

The procession continued until I finally perceived my greatest horror...

... Shauna! Her face and naked body were all battered and bruised. She dangled like a marionette, hanging from the thick branch of an enormous tree that would soon hold yet another innocent "witch."

A Game of Cards
by Joan Salter

It was a winter's night in 1946 that Mr. John Holt alighted from his train at Padiham, a tiny country station nestling in the chill of a seemingly deserted East Lancashire. He had travelled over from Widnes to do business with Roy Stafford of Grange Manor, an isolated mansion seemingly in the middle of nowhere if the map was anything to go by. However, Mr. Stafford's letter of invitation had promised a car would be sent to meet him at the pre-arranged time of arrival.

He had the carriage to himself for several stops before arriving, and was the only passenger to disembark when he did. Alone, he stood on the cold windy platform and looked around. It was deserted, except for himself and an old station master who was locking up the waiting room. He called the man over, gave his name and asked if there was a Mr. Stafford's car waiting for him.

"No, sir. There hasn't been a car here," the old man replied.

"Oh.... Well could you get hold of a taxi for me please?"

"I'm sorry sir, but we don't get many people coming here so we have no taxis."

"I see. Well, is there some sort of conveyance which would take me to Grange Manor?"

"I'm sorry sir, but you won't get anyone to take you at this hour of night."

Not entirely surprised at this news, John shrugged his shoulders. "Oh well, I'll just have to walk. How far is it?"

"Two miles sir. Follow this road as far as the crossroads, then turn left and keep straight on, you can't miss it."

John nodded, adding "Thanks, I'll start now. Will you have my luggage sent to me tomorrow?"

"Yes sir, I'll see to it for you. Goodnight sir."

So, John set out, pulling his coat collar a little higher around his ears, and setting his hat more firmly on his head. It was a wild night, with a high wind and had started to snow lightly.

John could feel flakes stinging his eyes and face as he walked. He was a young man, not yet 30, and strong and healthy, so two miles did not seem very much to him. He had also taken the precaution of carrying a torch.

He eventually reached the crossroads and paused for breath before turning left and pushing on once more. Stumbling along in the inky darkness, and only using his torch when he needed it to conserve the batteries, he heard a strange creaking sound above the noise of the storm.

Switching on his torch, he saw the dark bulk of a house not far from where he was standing. The creaking sound was made by a rusty old gate swinging loose on its hinges in the wind.

By this time there was a heavy blizzard blowing, so John decided he would have to take shelter in the house. He walked up the overgrown path and paused at the front door.

The whole place looked unused and neglected. John pushed the door which opened slowly and admitted him into a large dark hall.

Closing the door behind him, he had the uncanny feeling of someone standing in the shadows, watching him. Silently, he moved forward to another door, carefully opened it and stepped into a large room that looked as though it had not been in use for years.

To his surprise, there was a wood fire burning in the grate and looked recently lit. Taking off his coat, he stretched out his hands to the warm glow. Whoever his absent host was they certainly extended a hospitable welcome to this cold, weary traveller. Here he could shelter until the blizzard subsided and be on his way.

The comforting crackle of the fire was suddenly interrupted by the opening of a door. John looked round and stood within the frame of the doorway a man dressed in a suit of old fashioned clothing and carrying a lamp. Walking into the room, the glow from his light unveiled a long face that elongated down into as pointy chin and the thinnest of lips. He looked at John with strangely malevolent eyes, and he felt a cold fear strike him.

The stranger went over to the table, placing his lamp upon it. In a deeply velvet voice, he then said, "Do you play cards?"

With this strange question John stared at him in surprise then stuttered, "Y-yes" in a rather small voice. The man produced a deck of playing cards from inside his jacket and, sitting down at the table, motioned John to the other chair. He then dealt the cards out and announced, "The game is poker and we play for high stakes."

"I'm not carrying much in the way of money," John pleaded, sensing this was not a man to be refused.

"I speak not of money," his host explained. "The wager is quite simple. If you win the best of three hands, you may leave here unharmed. If you lose, I will possess myself of your soul."

John shook his head. "I'm sorry?"

"You heard me correctly," the stranger affirmed. "And a refusal to play will be instant forfeit" he added, anticipating John's next thought.

With seemingly no choice, John nodded and began to play the strangest game of his life, for his life.

The stranger cut the cards and dealt out five each, the two men played on silently. As each built up their hand and attempted to out bluff one another, John's grew face wet with perspiration and fear while the stranger remained grim and menacing.

John managed to achieve the first hand with a full house and, with the cards re dealt, embarked on the second with greater confidence. It proved misguided when his opponent trumped with four of a kind. Everything now rested on the third game.

The hand was soon nearing showdown and John waited, having kept outwardly calm so as not to give the stranger advantage, held his breath. If the card he'd just been dealt proved higher he would go free. If not...

He turned it over. It was an Ace.

Roy Stafford was awakened by the thunderous knocking on his front door. He jumped out of bed, ran downstairs and reached the door just before the half-dressed butler. He opened it and John, looking a lot older than they last met, stumbled inside and fell unconscious to the floor.

It took a large brandy to revive him. John had been sat in an armchair by a newly lit fire roaring to life. The butler was crouched over him in his dressing gown, holding the nearly empty glass in his hand, his employer overlooking from behind. He then turned his head to look at Mr. Stafford who nodded in silent instruction.

The butler stepped back as Mr. Stafford came forward and slightly bent until more face to face with his guest. "How you are feeling Mr. Holt?" John's voice croaked "The car... Didn't come."

"It was delayed by a fallen tree on the road. When my driver eventually reached the station, the porter told him you had set off walking. He followed the road back hoping to pick you up, but saw neither hide nor hair of you."

"The house... I was in the house."

"What house was that, old chap?"

John struggled with his distraught memory. "Large dark house, just after the crossroads, stood on its own."

Mr Stafford looked at the butler who shrugged his shoulders. He then turned back to John.

"Never mind, you can tell us in the morning. Your luggage was brought back and is in your room. Nowell will take you up and make you comfortable." He nodded at the butler who gently took John's arm, "If you would like to come with me, sir."

Exhaustion ensured John slept deeply, before being awakened next morning by the butler with a tray of tea. Standing at the wash basin, he looked at the mirror to find his face drawn and hair contained strands of grey, like he had just woken from many years of sleep.

Joining Mr. Stafford for breakfast, he sat opposite him at the table and his host enquired as to how he was now feeling. He then asked what had happened, but John just shook his head. "If I told you, you would not believe me." In the cold light of day, he was already beginning to question if the strange events of the previous night had actually taken place.

At John's behest, the business was undertaken with expedience so that he could return to Widnes later that same day. As evening fell, Mr. Stafford's driver began driving him back to Padiham to catch the evening train. Reaching the crossroads, John's eyes scanned the landscape in puzzlement before asking "Where's the house that stands around here?"

"No house here, none for miles," the driver replied.

John Holt sat back with a sigh in his breath. Wherever it had vanished, the house had taken something of him with it.

The Tale of Thrimblenorton
by Kevin Patrick McCann

My Mother was an Irish witch and for the three nights of
every full moon, she'd change into a she-cat. It is how she
met my Father, who was actually a cat.

She delivered me herself, which was just as well, as I was
born kitten and, unusually, a litter of one. I grew quickly
and only shifted to human form at sunrise. Now I can
change at will-Mother taught me- but overall, I prefer
being a cat.

After three human years I longed to see what was on the
other side of the hill. In cat years, I was fully grown and
ready to leave the nest. In fact, if I'd been all cat, I'd have
left long before. It was my human side held me back; that
and not wanting to leave Mother.

But we both knew it was time. The morning I was leaving
(I was in human form as we'd decided that was best) she
opened the cottage door and there was a large black tom
cat – I knew he was a tom by his song; which is what we
call his scent- sitting under the lavender bush washing
his whiskers.

Mother smiled down at me saying, "This is your Father,
Three Moons Rising. He'll travel some of the way with
you. He knows the wide world, you don't."

I blinked slowly at him–which is only good manners- and
asked, "Why's he called Three Moons Rising?"

You might think it odd that I didn't ask where he'd been for the last three years or why he'd turned up now to kitten-care me; and myself full grown. But cats never do. We don't wonder how we got somewhere, we just make the best of it.

I heard his deep voice inside my head- I'll say *said* in future; it's less of a mouthful, "Because of these!" and he lifted back his chin, stretched his neck and displayed three perfect round white moons rising up from his breast to his throat.

"They're beautiful," I said and then added, "Will I call you Father or Three Moons Rising?"

"Best call me neither in case you let fall in front of humans. Call me Tibbs. Humans will think it's just a cat name but *we'll* know it's our secret word for Father."

I promised Mother I'd come back every chance I got and then she'd bumped her nose tip against mine, gone back inside the cottage, firmly closing the door. Cats hate long goodbyes.

So off we set into a fine summer morning. Our progress was slow as Tibbs needed to stop, wash and then sleep every few miles, so in the end I carried him. It made sense. My legs were longer than his. My human legs that is. We avoided lanes and villages and when we did have to pass close to humans, we would glamour them so none would spy us.

I had both human food – soda bread and goat's cheese – and dried fish for Tibbs. We drank from streams and towards sunset, came to the hem of a forest.

My skin was beginning to itch. I always changed at sunset; I slept better for one thing. I put Tibbs down and as the sun vanished, shifted back to a cat. If you're wondering what happened to my clothes, the answer is, they turned back into fur. When I take human shape, my fur becomes clothes; when I shift back to a cat, they shift back to fur.

As soon as I was a cat again, it was like getting all my senses back. I could hear every individual sound clearly. Before, it was like listening through a wall. I could smell every song on the air and know one from another. My whiskers tingled with every movement of every living thing around me so I could have hunted blind if needs be. And though to your eyes all would now be black and colourless, I could see every colour there is and a few more besides.

Once the moon'd risen, we set out hunting and did well on field mice. Afterwards, we were crouched lapping from a stream, when we saw music in the distance. As it rose up into the night sky, it spun threads of colour that plaited into intricate knot patterns swelling like a poppy seed head about to burst.

But as more threads rose up out of the grass and shrubs around us, rushed into the sky and mingled with the music, my whiskers began tingling and when I turned round, I could see all the trees swaying though there wasn't a breath of wind in the air.

"It's the song of Herself; The Mother of Us All," Tibbs explained. "Let's get closer," and went down on his haunches before springing across the stream.

I followed but didn't quite clear it and ended up bedraggled, wet and miserable so naturally, wanted to sit down and groom.

"No time," said Tibbs firmly, "The night air'll dry you out." and set off at a run. I followed and by the time we reached the edge of a big clearing, I was bone dry. Tibbs was crouched low in the undergrowth so I crouched too.

The clearing was full of humans dancing around a huge fire. They were in couples, each back to back, hands held and looking at each other sideways on. At one end of the clearing were men and women playing musical instruments and at the other was a great pile of stones with a statue perched on top. It had a goat's body and a horned human head. A woman was bowing down before it.

"What's going on?" I asked Tibbs.

"A Sabbat," he explained, "They're a coven of humans who think they're witches and the woman is their Priestess."

I was about to ask him what a Priestess was when the music suddenly stopped and the dancers with it. The Priestess stood up, turned to face them and raising both arms chanted,

"What are Kings?"

"Tyrants!" came the loud response.

"What are Nobles?" she chanted.

"His familiars!"

"Who set them all over us?"

"Their Christian God!"

"Who do we worship?"

"Great Lucifer; Lord of Light and Liberty!"

I didn't understand a word of it and soon stopped listening anyway as I was aware of more movement behind me. I looked round and could see other humans- all male- carrying unsheathed swords and moving in.

"Witch-Finders," Tibbs warned me "Stay low and don't move."

The men were closer- close enough to hear their breathing- and I could see they had the clearing surrounded.

"When I say run," Tibbs said, "follow me."

There were men on either side of us but we stayed low so were safe as long as one of them didn't tread on a tail.

The one next to me raised his right hand and then brought it rapidly down shouting, "Now!" and all of them rushed into the clearing.

"Run!" Tibb shrieked and he was up the nearest tree with me no more than a heartbeat behind him. He settled on a lowish branch with me next to him.

The clearing was full of people, some screaming and trying to get away; others waving swords and killing them. The Priestess they took alive and soon all the others, except for one man, were dead.

"He must be the one who informed," Tibbs said. He must have seen I wasn't sure what he meant. "He betrayed them for money."

I blinked my understanding then we went back to watching the scene unfold.

One man, their leader presumably, walked over to where the woman was being held down by three of his men and said, "Take your pleasure then hang her."

He turned to the informer. The man's arms were still pinioned but he was clearly not afraid. The leader smiled at him but his smile was false.

"You've done well," he said but had to raise his voice as the woman was screaming so loudly, he paused and turning shouted, "Bind that bitch's mouth!"

He then turned back to the informer saying, "You'll be wanting your reward!" then nodded to one of his men who produced a knife and slit the informer's throat.

The men holding him let go, he fell to his knees clutching his throat before falling over sideways and gargling his last.

And then the whole scene faded. I looked to Tibbs for an explanation but instead of explaining Tibbs jumped down and I followed.

He sat back, scratched his ear furiously and then said, "We saw a future." I was still no wiser so he went on, "When we see a future we can sometimes change it. When we see a past, we can't."

"How can you tell one from the other?"

"Future pictures look solid. The past looks like ghosts."

"I've never seen a ghost."

"Oh you will Thrimblenorton," he purred, "you will."

It was starting to get light although all the birds were still silent. I was tired and Tibbs yawned widely in sympathy. "Let's sleep now," he said so we did.

* * *

Tibbs woke me with a soft bump on the nose and two freshly dead mice. I knew they were both for me as the way he was licking his teeth told me he'd already eaten.

I made short work of them and then walked back to the stream and drank.

"Now," said Tibbs once I was quenched, "let me explain. What we saw was a future and it was shown to us by the Mother of Us All," which is what we cats call the Creator, "and she showed us so we can change it."

"How can we do that?

"By finding the informer and stopping him," he then sat back on his haunches purring loudly at his own cleverness. .

"How will we find him?"

"Follow the stream downhill until we come to the nearest village. He'll most likely be there."

"Will I shift back to human-shape?"

"No, stay as you are; if we find the Priestess you shifting back might be just the thing to convince her you're telling the truth." He paused to give his flank a quick lick and then went on, "You'll have to do the talking. She's not really a witch so won't be able to hear my thoughts."

We set off downhill, keeping low and staying in the long grass and shadows as much as possible. It was a warm morning and there were butterflies everywhere so the urge to chase a few – not catch and eat mind, just chase – was almost overwhelming. Tibbs sensed it in me – cats sense moods the way human notice smells – so began talking.

"The humans we saw in the Future think they're witches and so did the ones who killed them…but they're not. Real witches like your Mother are rare and they never draw attention to themselves."

"Who's Lucifer?"

"Nobody," he said, "he doesn't exist."

"So why do they worship him?"

"Because they think he'll save them. They think he's going to appear one fine night, end all the bad in the world and then they'll all live happily ever after. They've no real hope and believing in Lucifer gives them some."

"What do the witch-finders believe?"

"Oh them," Tibbs said, "they're insane so who cares?"

I wanted to ask more but he set off again so I followed. I could smell wood smoke, faint at first but getting stronger; and then saw a thin stream of grey smoke rising from just beyond a copse at the other end of the field.

"If this is the Priestess' house," Tibbs said, "I'll know we're led and still meant to interfere. Be cautious though until we're sure."

Then he ran across the field and into the copse with me trailing. We emerged the other side to see a small cottage and a woman scattering food amongst some chickens.

And I could see the woman's face. It was the Priestess. .

"Shift to human form and beg a drink of water," Tibbs instructed me. "Tell her I'm nearby but you won't call me unless she gives permission. Tell her I won't attack her chickens."

"And then what?"

"And then," he said patiently, "I'll do the thinking and you'll do the talking."

With that, we stepped back into the shade of the copse, I shifted into human form, stepped back out again and called across to her, "Good day to you. Might a thirsty man beg a drink of water?"

She smiled at me, scattered the last of the chicken feed and said, "No need to beg. Of course you can and welcome."

"I have a cat," I said, "But I won't call him unless you give permission. He's well behaved," I added, "so won't attack your chickens."

She nodded, "In that case, you're both welcome."

So Tibbs and myself strolled across to meet her. As soon as the chickens saw Tibbs, they scattered but Tibbs was as good as his word and while I drank the mug of water she'd fetched me, he sat back on his haunches and purred.

"You a travelling man?" she asked and in my head, I heard Tibbs' reply which I repeated, "I am and I have a warning for you."

She looked at me, eyes narrowing and clearly not feared, "Warning or threat?"

"Warning," Tibbs thought and I repeated before shifting to a cat and then back to a human; when I'd resumed human form, she said, "Who are you?"

"No names," I said, "Just a warning." repeating Tibbs' words.

And Tibbs said, "Press your fingertips lightly to either side of her head, close your eyes, remember what we saw and she'll see it too." Then added, "Tell her she'll have to watch this to the end; say it's not pleasant but she needs to see."

I repeated his message and when I'd finished, she nodded then looked up at me - I was the taller by a good half-leg - and said "Go ahead."

When we'd done, she was pale and shaking. "Ryan!" she spat out the word angrily, "Tim Ryan. I should have guessed." She paused, "Come inside."

We followed her in. Tibbs settled in front of the turf fire and I sat down on one of the two stools by the fireplace.

She sat down on the other and said, "Tim Ryan's one of our coven and of late, he's pestered me with demands for certain...favours."

"And you refused him," I said echoing Tibbs...as I did for the rest of the conversation.

"I refused him and threatened to shun him if he didn't leave me alone. I knew he was angry but I didn't think he'd..."

"When's the Sabbat?" I asked.

"A month hence," she said, "so he can't have informed yet."

"How can you be sure?"

"I never tell the coven when and where the next Sabbat is going to be until the last minute; less chance of anybody letting slip then."

A man's voice from outside shouted, "Katy, are you there darling?"

"Talk of the devil," she said, "That's him now. Stay here and make sure he doesn't see you." then she got up and went outside.

Tibbs and myself glamoured him and watched from the doorway; Katy was all smiles and welcoming.

"Clever," Tibbs whispered.

"So Tim, what can I do for you this fine morning?" she was saying.

"Soften your heart," came his reply. "My only crime is to love you."

"I know," she said, "and I think I've been a bit hard on you."

He stepped forward, "Does this mean..." his voice trailed off and he gave her his best lost kitten in the snow that's just been found look.

I thought she'd laugh but to my amazement, she stepped forward and kissed him passionately on the mouth. Then pushing his hand away from her breasts said, "Come back at sunset and there'll be more where that came from."

Once he was out of sight, she spat on the ground and came back inside. "Time to cook a goose," she said draping a shawl round her shoulders. "Help yourself to cheese and bread," and off she went.

Tibbs curled up in front of the fire and fell asleep. After ten minutes of staring out of the window munching bread and cheese, I decided to join him. I stayed in human form though just in case Katy got back before I woke up. She thought I was all human and it was best things stay that way.

* * *

It was late afternoon when Katy got back and woke us both saying, "All's arranged," and then added, "you'll have no part in what's coming."

It wasn't long before we heard him shouting, "Katy, I'm here."

"Wait there," she shouted back and then to us, "I'll see you two later," before stepping outside.

* * *

She came back next sunrise carrying a basket. There was fresh mud on the hem of her dress and I was desperate to know what had happened; but I'd enough manners to wait until she was ready to tell. She threw Tibbs a dried fish from the basket and then handed me some kind of pie. Pork as it turned out.

While we both munched she said, "Tim Ryan's gone." She was acting calm but fooling no-one...except maybe herself.

I finished the pie and Tibbs swallowed down the last of the fish.

"Would you like any more?" she asked but before I had the chance to say, "Yes please!" I found myself echoing Tibbs' "No thanks; we've eaten our fill, you're safe so it's time we were off."

He paused a moment, adored her feet and then walked out with me following. We moved silently across the field and it was only when we'd reached the copse that Tibbs said, "Ask me."

"All right," I said, "what happened?"

"Look at the ground," he said, "What can you see? Shift to a cat, you'll see more."

I picked out two sets of tracks – a man's and a woman's – to begin with they were walking together but as they reached the edge of the copse, the woman began walking on tip-toe and the man following close behind doing the same.

"They were running," Tibbs explained, "him chasing her."

The trail came out of the copse, up the rise and into the forest. You could see how she'd paused so he almost caught up before running off again. It ended in a clearing that encircled a deep looking pond. Her tracks stopped by the pond's edge; so did his and they were facing each other.

More tracks came out of the bushes. These became mixed up with his and some of them were deeper and leading straight into the pond.

There was an empty bottle glinting in the sedge and giving off a fierce smell of drink and floating face up on the surface of the pond was an obviously dead Tim Ryan. I looked at Tibbs.

"Well," he said, "what happened?"

I sat back and thought. She'd run, staying in sight but just out of reach, led him here and let him catch her. Others had been waiting, grabbed him and drowned him; but why the bottle?

"So when he's found people'll think he fell in drunk," Tibbs explained.

If I'd been in human form, I'd have said something profound. But I was a cat so when I saw a butterfly land on a bush and then take off again, I forgot everything else and gave chase. Tibbs followed and we never went back that way again.

That was the first time I saw religion used to justify cruelty by humans. It wouldn't be the last.

A Secret Taken to the Grave
by Norbert Gora

In 1612 to Lancaster
The devil's retinue came
Black clouds of anxiety
Took the whiteness of the sky

Duel of the servants of darkness
Should be finished
By the grip of the choking noose
But at the gates of agony
Several mysterious words were said

A secret taken to the grave
Divided between eleven coffins
Hidden in the murkiness of oblivion
Waited, listening to the beating
Of absentminded clocks

The Curse of the Pendle Witches
by Chris Newton

"In memory of all those who suffered through prejudice and intolerance." Anna read aloud as they stepped from The Golden Lion and onto the pavement, light headed and slightly giddy from one too many spiced rums. She hadn't felt like they'd been in the pub very long, but the sun was already sinking beneath the adjacent rooftops, its remaining golden rays blinding against the blood red October sky. There was a definite chill in the air, a sign the lingering summer, which had seemed endless, had finally given way to autumn.

"Has that always been there?" She peered at the list of names on the bronze plaque on the side of the building.

"How can you not have noticed that?" laughed John.

She shrugged. "Is it something to do with the Pendle Witches?"

"Yes! How long have you lived here?" He regarded her incredulously.

"Too long." She rolled her eyes. "I can't remember. *That's* how long!" Anna had come to Lancaster University to study psychology and had failed spectacularly, dropping out halfway through her second year. Her parents had expected her to come back home, but the bar she'd been working in on weekends had offered her a full-time job, and there was Matt, of course. They were in a fairly intense relationship at the time. That had been enough to keep her in Lancaster. They'd grown apart eventually, at least that's what she told people. She tended to leave out the part involving her sleeping with his best friend. But that was all in the past, and Lancaster was her home now. It had become comfortable.

Too comfortable.

She had a decent job and good friends she went out with at weekends. Staying there was just... Easy. But the truth was, she was stagnating. Her twenties were disappearing like towns through the window of a train; glimpsed but not truly experienced. She needed to do something about that.

"It's time to leave this town."

They walked down the cobbled hill, towards the bus station, swaying slightly with intoxication. They passed a theatre, and into Stonewell Square, a junction of several streets with a memorial fountain sitting in its centre. The combination of heels and cobbles caused Anna to stumble slightly, and John held out his arm for her to steady herself. She giggled, linking her arm in his and resting her head affectionately on his shoulder. He felt his heartbeat quicken and needed to catch his breath, secretly savouring the scent of her hair; coconut shampoo mingled with smoke from the pub's fireplace. She smiled up at him and they looked into one another's eyes for longer than might be considered usual. The lyrics from a Smiths song tumbled unbidden into his mind. *And in a darkened underpass I thought, Oh God, my chance has come at last, but then a strange fear gripped me and I just couldn't ask.*

Anna laughed and looked away. Of course, he thought, she was so relaxed with him physically because she just didn't see him in that way. Not anymore. They were strictly platonic.

After Matt had found out about their indiscretion, they had insisted that it meant nothing, just a drunken hook up, as though that somehow made it acceptable. Forgivable, even. It had been much more than that to John. He assumed she had felt the same way, but they'd spent so many years since that night as 'friends' that it seemed to have stuck. And now she was leaving, heading to Manchester to study Fine Art. If he didn't tell her now he never would. He suspected that had been it, the moment she'd taken his arm and held his gaze, and he'd missed it.

She was no longer looking at him, staring instead over his shoulder at a poster on display outside the theatre. "Jesus. This town really does have a serious witch fixation, doesn't it?"

He turned to see what she was looking at, a poster for a play depicting the black silhouette of a cross against a crimson backdrop of skeletal branches. The title of the play was *Sabbat*.

"Well it's history, isn't it? London has Jack the Ripper and Lancashire is..." He fumbled for the right term. "Witch County."

"Still, I don't see why they have to stick the names of the witches on all the pubs."

"It's not all the pubs! Just The Golden Lion! That's where they had their last drink."

"What?"

"It's true. It's where people would be allowed one final drink on their way to the gallows." He pointed up the road towards Gallows Hill, where the green dome of the Ashton Memorial rose above slate rooftops, through the distant foliage of the wooded park.

"The pub's not even that old."

"Well, not the building, no, but the pub that was at the site before it." He said as they walked away from the square, passed the stone fountain illuminated by the glow of fairy lights from the window of a nearby restaurant. "My brother always used to say that they cursed Lancaster before they died."

"Right…"

"He said that no one can ever leave. Once you move here, that's it. That's the curse of the Pendle Witches."

"Aren't curses supposed to make you erupt into boils and stuff?" she sniggered.

"I think it's kind of poetic, if you think about it. I mean, they were brought here… But they didn't get to leave, did they?"

"Well, I hate to ruin your story, but I'm about to break the curse."

"It's just a legend. I didn't say I believed it," he grumbled.

They crossed the road, past the shopping arcade, past a bakery on the corner whose window was decorated bat-shaped paper garlands above a tray of gingerbread ghosts, and towards the bus station.

The air was acrid with the smoke from a distant bonfire, and the castle hung in the sky above, a sentinel observing the city that sprawled out beneath it. It was funny, Anna thought. The witch trials of 1612 did not seem like reality. They were something that had happened in another world, or in a film, and had nothing to do with Lancaster and its pubs, shops and theatres. Until you looked up. Until you saw the castle, unchanged in four hundred years. One could well believe there were witches rotting in its dungeons, even now.

"Anyway, what about you?" She asked.

"What about me?"

"Hopes? Desires? Ambitions? What are you going to do with the rest of your life?"

"Dunno," he lied. He had plenty of hopes, but they all involved her.

Without warning, the twenty or so pigeons gathered about the entrance to the station to peck at scraps suddenly took simultaneous flight, as though startled by something unseen, and all about them were dirty grey wings fluttering insistently.

"Woah!" she stopped him in his tracks as the birds dispersed.

"What's up?"

"Déjà vu. Weird!" She shuddered. "I could have sworn I knew that was going to happen."

"Apparently you get déjà vu when it takes your brain longer than usual to process something. Like, your eyes have already seen it, so by the time you've acknowledged it, you already remember seeing it on some subconscious level. But it's all, like, split second so you're not really aware of it."

"No, I'm just psychic." She poked her tongue out at him.

As they approached the station's automated doors, they saw a beggar crouched by their side. Matted hair poked from beneath a ragged woollen hat and framed a grizzled face of sores and dirt.

"Spare any change please?" he croaked as they neared him. John instinctively reached into the pocket of his jeans.

"John!" Anna glared at him. "He'll only spend it on drugs." John felt his hand obediently sliding back out of his pocket.

"Sorry mate, no cash," he mumbled.

"Got a light?" the beggar rasped as they were walking away. Ignoring Anna's reproachful glare, John turned back, proffering his lighter. The grubby man fumbled in the pocket of his tatty parka for what was, essentially, a butt, flattened and dirty. He held it between his thumb and forefinger, almost burning his fingertips in his attempt to light it. John couldn't bear to watch any longer.

"Here." He produced a packet of menthols from his jacket.

"I once gave my soul to a Thing like a Christian man," said the beggar as he inhaled.

"I'm sorry?"

The ragged man laughed throatily. "One half of his coat black. The other brown."

"John, come on, I'll miss my bus..." Anna snapped, already beginning to walk away.

"Spare any change please?" The man held up a polystyrene cup and rattled what meagre coinage it contained.

"Sorry mate..." John held up his palms apologetically as he turned his back.

"His name was Tibb." The beggar chuckled his death rattle, its hacking, mocking sound reverberating throughout the station.

Anna slid her arm into John's once more as they approached stand number Six.

"Manchester?" an official looking man in a high-vis jacket asked.

"Yeah."

"Sorry, air brake light's on. We're waiting for a replacement service. Gonna be at least an hour."

Anna's shoulders sagged. "Great."

John shot her a sideways glance. "Pub?"

"You read my mind."

As they retraced their steps, away from the smell of petrol fumes and stale urine, they noticed a ripple of commotion. Ahead, a semicircle of people were gathered by the entrance. Through the spectator's legs they saw the beggar, collapsed in a twisted heap on the concrete floor. Somebody was frantically calling an ambulance, whilst others were posing for morbid selfies.

With a terrible cry, he lurched up into an unnatural position, head lowered at a painful angle, shoulders bunched around his ears. Anna froze when she saw his face. The features on the left side were sagging as though he had suffered a stroke, his cheek drooping, the left corner of his lip curling downward and leaving a trail of spittle oozing down the front of his coat, the skin around his left eye sunken to reveal the red raw flesh below a bloodshot eyeball.

He extended his functioning arm towards her through the gaggle of onlookers as he screamed. "Any who practice witchcraft, enchantments or sorcery whereby any shall die will die as felons, without sanctuary or benefit of the clergy!" A distant wailing heralded the approach of an ambulance as the beggar crumpled to the floor once more and was silent.

"Well, that wasn't remotely disturbing." Anna gave John a wide-eyed look as they backed slowly away from the spectacle.

Upon their return to The Golden Lion, Anna saw the plaque listing the names of the accused and wondered now how she had ever missed it. Inside, John ordered a pint of *Black Cat* and a spiced rum and they took their seats, nestling into cracked leather armchairs opposite a lit fire which hissed and crackled in the grate. The sleepy room smelled of whisky and wood smoke.

"You want a try?" He offered her his beer.

She wrinkled her nose suspiciously. "It's not gonna be one of those hoppy ones that taste like straw and... Fairy Liquid, is it?"

"No, It's a dark mild. It's malty," he added unhelpfully. She took a tentative sip before swiftly wincing in disgust.

"Eurgh! It tastes like soil!"

"It's nice," he laughed. "Just takes at bit of getting used to."

They sat in silence for a few moments, mesmerised by the flames, as words unsaid churned in the pit of John's stomach.

"I'm really gonna miss you," he blurted suddenly.

"I'll miss you, too." She smiled tenderly, before laughing. "Come on, it's not like I'm leaving the country."

"I know. I know. It's just, ever since..." The words died in his throat.

Anna glanced at her phone. "Come on. I need to get going." She said, placing her empty glass definitively on the table before them, its rim bearing a ghostly pink imprint where her lips had touched it. "Don't want to miss my bus."

"Yeah. Course." He downed his pint and pulled his coat on as they made for the exit. "Cheers!" He nodded to the landlady as he placed their empties on the bar.

"See you next time." The silver haired woman smiled from behind the pumps, watching as he stepped out into the crisp autumnal evening to join Anna, who was staring at the plaque on the wall.

"In memory of all those who suffered through prejudice and intolerance." She read aloud. "Has that always been there?"

"How can you not have noticed that?" laughed John.

She shrugged. "Is it something to do with the Pendle Witches?"

"Yes! How long have you lived here?" He regarded her incredulously.

"Too long." She rolled her eyes. "I can't remember. *That's* how long! It's time to leave this town."

As Witches
by Chrissy Derbyshire

Pendle
It grows black moss on the tongue
If spoken like a spell.
Tongue twined around a tree,
Close around its green heart.
Stronger than vine,
Strong as devil's fingers,
If you speak it well.

Pendle
It grows a wood in your mind
And she lives there,
The one you wish for
In those ordinary days
When you are ordinary
And good
And all grown up.

She lives there,
Nests in a dark corner
Of a hollow house
In the imagined past
Of an imagined wood
Where you never walked
Never made footprints in tree-dust and needles,
But your mind flies there
When you loosen your grip.

Chattox, they called her.
Or Demdike?
The stories you read long ago,
And little details pierce through
Like long needles through clay,
But it is daytime
And the dishes
And the washing
And the child calling...

The child.
She made a witch of her child.
One of them did.
Both of them did?
It doesn't matter which.
You could take your little girl
And in a devil's handshake
Pass like a bribe the business card
Of Old Hornie.

And then in a quiet moment
Of insubordination
She might call that number –
Long distance, downwards –
And escape.

Chattox muttered soundlessly,
Moth-wing lips fluttering,
Whisperwhispers, smokelike, rising.
You imagine men would crawl
To drink in clear air under the enchantment,
Having been forced at school
To watch a PSA on keeping safe
In the event of witchcraft.

You do not wish to harm,
Nor especially to sign away your soul,
But once in a way
To be weird,
To be outside,
To be other,
To be talked about behind your back
With justifiable fear...

For that you might just shed your skin,
Husk on the kitchen floor with discarded clothes
And fly new as a babe
To Malkin Tower
To taste a crumb
Of what it is
That gets women hanged
As witches.

Phantasmagoria
by Shannon Fries

Here I am, once again, walking a lonely path, leaving a place I hoped to call home. I am glad there is a moon tonight, although she is an old moon, waning, but still bright enough to light my way. But I am not alone, Pip is with me. My sweet puss, who has always been by my side, helped dry my tears, kept me warm. She is old now, skinny and slow, and her beautiful long grey fur is becoming dull and lifeless. But I am thankful she is still with me, the last of anyone I can call family.

But once, once I did have a family, and hopes for so much more. My mother was a shining constant of my childhood. She lived in a small village in the North, near the wildness of the Yorkshire moors and the great hill dominating the roof of the county. She always spoke of her village in hues of blue. She loved my father there. They came together at an autumn harvest festival, he a lesser son of a lesser son, destined for a life in the church. But still the manor's son, and as such was a part of the village life, so their love was kept secret through the long dark winter.

When spring came burgeoning in, so too my mother's own fertility started to show, I was growing quickly inside her. The master soon found out about his son's dalliance and packed him off to a monastery far to the south, never to be seen by my mother again. Her grief was complete and so too the land surrounding the village became forlorn. With summer came a terrible drought that lasted for months. The farm animals had little to eat and soon dried up, and lost any babes they were carrying. Soon a sickness befell most of the villagers and the whispering began. My mother's grief had not gone unnoticed and she was soon blamed for the woes of the village. The night they came for her she fled into the nearby hills with me heavy inside her, with only the clothes on her back.

I was born soon after, in a thicket of Rowan trees. Born before my time, but born strong. Mother used to say that I came early so she wouldn't be lonely anymore. She made a home for us wherever she could; a cave, a Pine forest, the outskirts of a village. She made a living selling herbs and potions made from things her wisdom harvested in the forest. I grew quickly and she taught me many things such as how to find food and herbs in the woods, how to make medicines, treat wounds, find water. She also taught me of the animals in the woodland and how they can warn you of impending storms and unseen dangers. Many a little creature found its way into our home, to be cured of a broken wing or some other injury. There were always field mice or newts or some other little orphan in my apron pocket that I would care for until the time would come for them to go off on their own.

That is how Pip came to me. One day I followed my mother to a nearby village where she was going to try and sell some of her simples. She had left me in the woods at our camp, but my curiosity got the best of me. Behind the stalls of the market place, following the sounds of laughter, I came across some boys throwing stones at this little grey puff of fur. The kitten couldn't have been more than a few weeks old and all alone. Thankfully the boys' aims weren't very good and only a few glancing blows had struck the poor creature so far. Red filled my vision and although I weighed no more than a bag of grain, and the boys were much bigger than I was, I ran in screeching, tearing and scratching. So wild was my assault that they were soon driven off.

From then on Pip has been by my side, my truest friend. When my mother arrived back at camp later that afternoon she found me with the injured kitten. She looked at me strangely and told me about some boys that had been playing near an old manor building that afternoon when the stone walls caved in and killed them all. That night we packed and moved on.

As I grew older we decided to settle in a beautiful little village we found situated above a little cove far to the west, where many of the villagers would fish from their little coracle boats. There was an empty cottage at the edge of the town's boundary. Its roof was gone and there was no glass in the windows, but there was a sturdy fire chimney that drew clean and there was a well packed earthen floor. We slowly repaired the hovel and made it into a home, my first. We planted a garden, and traded for a couple of chickens and a goat. We made a good living and many of the villagers relied on us to cure their ills and mishaps. It was a happy time for us and I blossomed.

* * *

During my sixteenth spring boys started to notice me, and I shyly noticed them back, one in particular, the miller's son. A tall boy with brown hair and gold lit eyes. He would leave wildflowers on my doorstep and we would run off to the woods together, or meet in his father's hay loft. I can still feel the hay scratchy on my skin, sticking to our sweaty bodies as our inexperienced touches led to bolder embraces. My heart was fuller than I ever imagined it ever could be. It was the most beautiful and abundant summer of my life. The fields produced more food than ever before; the trees were laden with fruit, and the nets of the fisherman were so filled with sea creatures that they could hardly pull them into their boats. It was a season of plenty. And with all seasons, there came an end.

The miller soon found out about us, one day he caught us in the barn, our clothes loose and hay in our hair. He chased me out and cuffed his son, and I could hear his father yelling all the way through the fields. The next day when I saw my boy, he was standing in the market with some of his fellow friends. He wouldn't look at me. He wouldn't even talk to me, and his friends started to jeer when I wouldn't leave. Then all of a sudden he turned to me with dead eyes and said I meant nothing to him. He was going to marry another.

Tears blurred my eyes as I ran all the way home and my heart felt torn from my chest. When I reached the safety of my yard even the sky opened up with rain and wind as if it too felt my pain and sadness. For days I wouldn't speak or eat, but stayed in my loft or wandered the shoreline with my ever faithful Pip by my side. Sadness soon gave way to anger. What was wrong with me? Was I unworthy of love? or was I mistaken in who I gave my heart to? He was the one who was wrong and broken. He was the one that should feel the pain. I used my anger to build a wall around my heart and went home.

The very next day I heard some women weeping in the square, the miller's son had fallen from the hayloft in his father's barn and was impaled on one of the sharp forks used for haying. My beautiful boy was dead.

They started to avoid my mother and me after that. Less and less people would buy our wares or come to us with their troubles. My mother grew worried but never said anything.

I should have read the signs, I should have known evil was not far away. There were whisperings and looks, but still I didn't suspect. People have never been very friendly to us, certainly they came to us to help them, but there was never any true friendship anywhere we tried to make a home, so I thought nothing of it.

One morning my mother woke me early, she handed me a basket and asked me to go and fill it with Rowan berries and bark. The nearest grove of Rowan trees was on the other side of the far hills and I would be gone all day and into the night. Always a dutiful daughter, I took some bread and cheese and with Pip at my side I headed out into the grey dawn. Mother kissed me and held me close for a moment, and then let me go.

As I knew, the errand kept me all day, and I didn't return home until well after dark. The cottage itself was dark, with only the embers in the grate glowing for light. Mother wasn't there, but I wasn't worried. How many nights has mother been gone in the past to assist in a birth or help with an illness? I wrapped my blanket around me and settled to wait for her by the fire.

I must have nodded off because all of a sudden Pip shot off of my lap with a yowl, her hair on end, and raced under the table. I looked towards the door and saw a light, not a regular light from a candle, but a glowing, golden light, dancing near the entrance like a will o' the wisp. The light slowly took form and there was my mother, looking so sad. She tried to speak but no sound came out. However, her voice was clear in my head as she mouthed the words

"Run...flee! Save yourself, my daughter!"

I felt her love for me, and her fear which was telling me I had to leave. She was gone forever, but shines as a light in my memory. She will always live within me and within the brook burbling in the sunshine, and the dragonflies in the field...

* * *

My feet aren't tired although I have been walking this path for a long time. The moon is still in the sky but

77

sinking quickly to the west. I am approaching a clearing that I can't see, but I can feel it somehow, a large open space with the sky looking down. A fire burned there recently, a large fire, the remains filling the center of the clearing. I move closer and the embers are still smoldering in some places along with other things... bones.

There are bones mixed in with the ash and debris, human bones. Someone was burned here and I shiver with the thought. As I look near the edge where the fire had only barely scorched the grass, I notice something shine in the dim light. It is a small brass broach, the broach my mother had given me on my thirteenth name day, as her mother had given it to her when she came of age. What is it doing here? I reach down to pick it up and my hand passes right through it. Confused, I look at my hand and notice that it is slightly transparent. Scared and bewildered I look up at the sky above me and see a star. All at once I feel a part of the star, a part of everything. I can feel the sap in the trees moving sluggishly through their limbs, I can feel the flowers asleep at the edge of the meadow, and I feel the grass growing, already repairing the scared earth at my feet. I am a part of the breeze that is blowing, dancing down the valley and into the clearing, blowing away the scent of decay and hatred; I feel the heartbeat of an owl, alert in the trees, I am it and it is me.

I look back toward the place of burning and find myself looking at it from a height somewhat above. There is little Pip lying still in the grass at the edge of the fire, so small and still. Has she left me too? No, here is her muzzle rubbing my hand. I feel a lightening, a deep sense of peace, I am no longer troubled, I am no longer alone, I look up at the waning moon and I am no longer...

Never, truly, the end....

The Forest of Pendle
by Juleigh Howard-Hobson

Let us speak of tree hung curses,
White bone on sun bleached limbs.
Charm bags, blood stained and fixed to
brushwood.
Runes cut in low unknown branches, root
etched in ash.
A scarlet strand tied to Rowan twigs.
Haw berries threaded round and round an
Oak.

Let us speak of bark bound magic. Nine iron
nails embedded in a yew.
Hexes hid in hollows.
Dark Sigils carved in stumps,
In logs, in places that lay unseen,
Undisturbed beneath mold and moss.
This magic holds. Time erases nothing here.

Let us speak of ages old enchantments,
Of witches' spells faintly sung
And heard still, close to where they all were
hung.

Beneath Malkin Tower
by Kathleen Halecki

Cleworth, Parish of Leigh, Lancashire, 1597

The Bible fell from Reverend Darrell's hands as he felt
his fingers being crushed by something unseen. He
patiently retrieved it from the floor understanding that
this was an ongoing battle against evil forces trying to
exert their power over the seven in the room. He was not
surprised that it was here in Lancashire; it was well
known amongst the clergy that it was a dark corner of
the kingdom, hopelessly backwards, full of ignorance,
denied access to the light of Jesus Christ, and like much
of the West, notorious for witchcraft. The people spoke of
fairies and water sprites in hushed tones, saw boggarts
in every hall and perched on every gate, and believed
that hobgoblins existed in the forest of Pendle. He had
only been in the county but a few days and witnessed
their superstitious rituals; on every house a horseshoe
was nailed above the door, and farmers offered milk to
the roots of a tree to preserve the power of a spell. Even
the father of two of the children present, Nicholas
Starkie, turned to a conjurer first. Trying to battle Satan
with Satan, he thought when beseeched to come, they
should have known better. The only cure for possession
was by fasting, the recitation of Psalm 51, readings from
the Gospel of John, and consistent prayer until the
demons released their hold.

The child, Anne, lay gasping on the floor as she convulsed, her small feet hitting the wood of the floors with a thumping sound, her face contorting to a grimace. She began to feel the sense of being overtaken, of being swallowed by something she thought of as the Other. Sometimes she would catch a glimpse of it, and she knew the six others with her in the room saw it as well. For some, it came as a foul creature with half a face, long shaggy hair, with broad hands and black coven hooves. Other times it appeared as a misshapen man, grotesque to behold. She witnessed with her own eyes the fits her brother but a year older, John, experienced when his nightmare plagued him. He often cried out that it was the "Shriker" from the forest that came as a large black dog dragging an enormous chain which it would attempt to wrap around his body.

The Other pushed back against her thoughts to gain control, angry the girl would not speak its name. If she would but call its name, it could overtake her; younger bodies were harder to take as they fought against it in their fear. It was much easier to be given permission to become a familiar, to be as one with the human it possessed, for those who were older understood the power they would obtain. Now it turned to look at the men in the room from the eyes of the girl as they began to recite from their holy book.

What fools, it thought. For as long as the lands existed, the brethren lived and would continue. Had this man learned nothing from the last attempted exorcism in Lancashire but ten years past? That priest, Father William, tried to banish them as well but he was cast into prison as a fraud. Even now he languished in a dreary castle without his freedom, his religion castigated and condemned. It felt a sense of pleasure at the thought. Even if he was unable to hold this girl, or its brethren take the other humans, it could still unleash its vengeance upon them all. The roots of the brethren ran deep and were spread afar across the land. Their time was coming and their numbers were swelling.

Reverend Darrell nodded to Reverend More and Master Dickoms, who both turned to Psalm 51 and in unison, began;

"Have mercie upon me, O' God, according

to thy loving kindness, according

to the multitude of thy compassions..."

Finally, after two hours of battle, the demons departed, but not before a terrible howling and shrieking. Blood poured from the mouths and noses of the seven, and witnesses watched in horror as a black mist came from out of their mouths only to disappear in a flash of fire. The seven then quieted themselves, their eyes tightly shut, while those around them praised God for their deliverance.

Reverend Darrell closed his Bible, but an unsettling feeling began to overtake him. Although he knew that the demons would try to possess one last time – for they always returned in their attempts to bribe and entreat – he felt that he had met with a terrible enemy and one that would not take the loss of seven souls lightly. He felt a shadow fall upon him, and wondered at the things to come.

* * *

Malkin Tower, near Forest of Pendle, Lancashire, 1612

Reverend Darrell adjusted his broad hat to shield his face, although he doubted any would recognize him. It was not just the years that changed him, but the hardship of life. Arrested shortly after the exorcism of the Seven of Lancashire, along with Reverend More, he was held for years, verbally abused by his enemies who denounced them as a couple of "cousining hypocrites" denying their ability to exorcise demoniacs. Eventually set free, he was stripped of his ministry and gone into hiding aided by like-minded clergy who understood the very real danger England faced, and to avoid further charges laid against him by those under the power of the devils of Lancashire.

He knew who, or at least what, was to blame for this misery. That same haunting presence he felt that night. He now truly understood the evil that held this county in its grasp. Rumors of witches persisted over the years, with Satan's Sabbath said to be held at this very place he now stood, Malkin Tower. This was the source of witchcraft now overtaking England. He had no doubt that in Pendle the dark forces were growing. He needed to find a way to destroy the hold over those who lived in this God-forsaken place and stop them from working their maleficium against innocents.

The talk in town was of the arrest of a number of witches, including the ones who made their abode in Malkin Tower. Old Demdike and her children even now were locked up in Lancashire gaol speaking freely of their familiarity with spirits. He was sure the answers were to be found in the grim, crumbling ruin before him. There was no telling the age, although he guessed that it was very old from the masonry. Inside, he was shocked by the meanness of the conditions under which they lived. As he lit the stubs of the candles above the fireplace, he could see raggedy bedclothes in various shades of mildewed grey were the only source of covering against a winter chill. The sparse furnishings seemed as old as the dwelling itself, rickety and lopsided, and ready to fall apart if used. The floor was stone but covered with dirt and strewn with hay.

As he stood there in the semi-darkness, he spied a large black cat with eyes like gold buttons staring at him from a crevice in the wall. It let out a loud hiss before disappearing under the bed. Believing it to be a familiar, he followed, only to see the creature vanish down a large hole only visible once he got down on hands and knees. Inching closer, he peered over the edge to be met with a stone step and a sense of terror came over him as he listened. He could hear mutterings and murmurings, like whispers, and he pulled back in order to move the bed and reveal the hole. Lighting his candle, he could see the stairs went straight down into darkness. His heart began to pound at the thought, but he knew that what he sought was somewhere down in the dark hell of that abyss.

With a deep breath, he began his descent with one hand against a stone wall, the other shakily holding the candle. The whisperings seemed to grow louder with each precarious step and his head began to buzz with the sound. Finally, the last stair was reached and he was met with a long, dark tunnel along which he continued. Reaching the end, he lifted his light to look around and before him lay an enormous cavern with no end in sight. He wondered how such a thing could be found in England until realising he was under Pendle Hill itself. He heard the same hiss of the cat and could vaguely make out its shape. Standing next to it was a small furry creature which resembled something out of a child's nightmare, prompting his thoughts back to the seven he dispossessed so many years ago, and their visions. It did not move, but stared at him and he could feel its hatred even in the dim light. Then, from somewhere out in the cavern, came another sound that sent his blood running cold. A shadow passed over the flame, and he felt something brush across his cheek.

Moving his candle over, he looked down to see dozens of the creatures beginning to descend upon him and, slowly, he began to retreat back to the tunnel. From out of the cavern, he heard yet another sound, as if something larger was moving in the back and he forced his body to move faster than a man of middle age, sensing small claws reaching out to grab at his cloak. After an agonizing ascent up the stairs, he reached the top as something caught the edge of his boots and pulled him back down into the edge of darkness, calling his name.

He began to recite from the Gospel of John, and taking his candle, flung it down into the hole. Reaching for the remnants of the candles still left, he set fire to the bed as he flipped it over the hole as small wings began to appear. Taking whatever was combustible in the room, he fed the flames as he called upon the protection of God's mercy and salvation from the evil that was before him. The flames began to grower higher and higher, catching on to the hay on the floor and spanning out across the old dried furnishings. From within the fire Darrell heard the roar of the creature from the cavern as stones from the floor were lifted and he caught a glimpse of the horror the seven experienced. The figure was man-like, but half of the face was twisted, with long locks of raven hair that fell over to one side and he saw a glimpse of cloven hooves beneath its dark robes. It opened its mouth to shout his name as the flames began to rise and Darrell backed away before the large hands could touch him.

Reaching into his vest, he drew out the papers provided to him by his associates. Drawn from the earliest of texts, the spells were intended to exorcise the demons of Lancashire. Dr. Dee labored over them even as he lay dying, knowing that the very soul of England was at stake. Throwing salt into the flames, Darrell began the incantation letting the power of the ancient words chain the horror before him. He already knew two of the names the witches provided freely during their depositions, Tibb and Fancie. In their over-confidence, they provided him with the power to close the very gate over which they lived. The demon tried to move out from the stones that were beginning to crumble to reach for him, but it was too late. The binding spell was already beginning to work, and as the fires grew hotter, the demon finally dissipated with an echoing roar.

He stood there for hours shaking as he watched the old stones finally topple over and the tower collapsed. As it lay smoldering, he covered the area with salt and crushed rose petals dipped in holy water. As the sun began to rise, he quoted one last time from the Gospel of John to keep that which was beneath Malkin Tower entombed forever.

"In the beginning was the Worde, and the Worde was with God, and that Worde was God. The same was in the beginning with God..."

* * *

Village of Barley, near Pendle Hill, 2011

The cat's skeleton was met with excitement by the archaeologists; trapped within the walls of a seventeenth century building near Pendle Hill, the possibility existed that the remains of Malkin Tower were finally coming to light. The bones of the creature lay before a sealed room long since covered over with earth. From the evidence it was clear that someone made their home there up until the nineteenth century living above the remains of the older building.

That Halloween, with Ouija boards in hand, the teenagers giggled as they made their way to the site. "I dare you guys," were issued by classmates who taunted their friends to contact the witches of Pendle, with one self-described Wiccan (but really a kid with no knowledge on the subject) proclaiming they knew "just the right spell" to use to call up the dead. Laying the board on the ground, they began to chant to any passing spirit in the vicinity.

The brethren stirred beneath the stones buried under the earth, listening and waiting. It would not be long before Lancashire would be theirs again.

On Pendleside
by Phil Howard

On Pendleside the kestrel dives;
Something dies, a death life's imperative dictates.
The heather, bracken, broom and all that lives in
Cat Hang Wood
This cycle drives. Natural virtue under lowering
skies.
But here it was not always so.
This brooding place is redolent of the blood
Of those sentenced to the stake,
Tortured, beaten, hung and burned;
The mob baying in the castle yard;
Not a martyr's death, but horror for horror's sake.

From hovels they have been dragged,
From huts, shacks, tents, churches,
Chateaux and ghetto tenements;
Witch, heretic and traitor, all put to the torch or
sword.
The scene replayed and replayed again:
The screams, the pleading, the cries;
The averted eyes of those obeying orders;
The huddle of humanity in the pen,
Herded like beasts to the slaughter;
The nervous laughter of the warders.

The hawk that dives on Pendle Hill is wired to kill:
A single mouse spared would erase ten million years;
Redraw the map of raptor evolution.
But the pyre is built as an act of will;
Choice, not instinct, ignites the fire.
For humankind Nature offers no absolution.

Maleficium
by Zowie Swan

Born of a whore

"I baptise thee Repentance! May the wickedness of thy parents be burdened upon thee in this life. Only through the grace of the Lord may you achieve absolution from this turpitude. For thou art a bastard little one and you'll never be anything more."

The folk of Newchurch shuddered at these hate-filled words, directed as they were to the pink, fleshy innocent in the Minister's arms. All had gathered in the stout little church to witness this most irregular baptism. Saint Mary's Chapel squatted, shame-faced, beneath the sinister skirts of Pendle Hill, known to the locals simply as 'The Hill' and culpable for so much darkness.

Nearly half a century had passed since the black shroud of Maleficium had haunted the county. England still reeled in the aftermath of a bloody civil war and the son of the beheaded King now sat on the throne. In recent times George Fox had even been blessed with a glorious vision whilst quaking in his God-fearing boots on this most infamous heathen hilltop. Order and light had been brought to the country. And yet... The people of Newchurch-in-Pendle remained fearful, cautious and over-wrought. They did not walk abroad in their county when dark fell. And if they must, they hastened.

Edward Lepage, the grey faced Minister, squinted sourly at the squirming, swaddled bundle in his arms and grimaced in disgust, as though whatever he held may taint him merely through the act of holding. As his lofty and dramatic words fell upon the ears of the parishioners, there was a distinct change in the atmosphere in the stark presbytery. The draughty chapel rippled with a susurration of unease. The gentry, in their respectable family pews, shifted slightly, almost imperceptibly, as though they found something distasteful but preferred to keep their silence. The rougher, simple folk, who made up the bulk of the congregation, audibly murmured their discomfort and a few were brave enough to shake their weathered heads in disbelief. Some of the older women were bolder still and chanced themselves to cluck loudly in disagreement. Yet, of all of those there gathered, only a ragtag party of three stepped forward to challenge the Minister for his improper attitude towards the babe in his arms.

"Mallie! Her name…her name is to be Mallie."

The voice belonged to a girl, no older than sixteen. Her face was pale and drawn, casting a veil of hardship over her otherwise lovely features. She was slightly built but her belly was still swollen, betraying to all within the church that the child was hers. Most of them, of course, already knew the scandal of her sin. They also knew that the father would not be manifesting to claim his bastard, if he knew what was good for him.

The girl was joined by an elderly woman, whose spine was beginning to twist and warp through old age. Their trio was completed by a diminutive man of early middle age, who owned a shock of untidy red hair. All three were dishevelled, unkempt and their clothes, as well as being raggedy, were also unseemly and fanciful. Where the rest of the congregation were swathed in demure blacks, humble browns, stoic greys and virginal whites, this unruly mob wore tattered reds, greens, blues and purples. The colours were greatly faded, but they still remained pronounced amongst the dull, drab garb of everyone else. Their clothes were antiquated and had fallen out of fashion a generation earlier. Spoils of war no doubt, after some aristocratic Cavaliers had lost their heads to Cromwell's axe. This exaggerated refinement, this bedraggled elegance made them fascinating, especially to the village children, who mistook them for mummers.

The queer trio stood defiantly, deliberately even, aside from everyone else, as the girl challenged the Minister. He looked upon them disdainfully and grimaced again, an act his face was often wanted to do.

"Mallie is not a Christian name!" he bellowed at her.

"Aye, it surely is! My Mothers cousin, her was called Mallie. That's who young 'un is named for. An' th'owd crone who lived by Sabden Brook, her was called Mallie an all, an her daughter. 'Tis a good Pendle name, is Mallie."

Mutterings of agreement rippled throughout the congregation, who watched on, dismayed by the scene before them. The Minister curled his lip and rolled his eyes.

"I care not what thy Mother's cousin was called! I know what thy Mother's cousin was! Furthermore, I will not be instructed to by a Device! Step back you insolent creature!"

The baby began to gristle and let out a pathetic mewling whimper, as is an infant's prerogative, but the Minister increased his grasp on the child in malice, causing it to cry even more. At this, the bent old woman shuffled stiffly forward and raised her face up to his, twisting her neck to one side like an owl as she did in order to look him in the eye. Despite her malformed frame she exuded an air of explicit authority and the church fell silent as it waited in anticipation of her next action.

"Mind yourself Edward. I brought you into this world. I've been there at the beginning of most of you gathered here an' I've been there at the end of many who've passed on before us. I'm sure I'll be there with a few more of you yet, when your time comes, to hold your hand in this life whilst you cross over into the next one."

The crowd again nodded in agreement at this, for it was as true as the hills themselves. Owd Mother Fortune had always been there. No doubt she'd be there to greet the Redeemer himself when the earth itself went cold. She held her benevolent gaze on the man whilst he considered his next move. He was tricksy this one and she knew she'd have to be canny when handling him. His predecessor, a defamer, fornicator and abuser, had been much easier to manipulate, for he had had a great deal to lose. This one was piety itself, which made him much more dangerous. The Minister eyed the old woman carefully. A beat passed. She spoke again.

"You will not harm that child. None will ever harm that child whilst there is breath in my body."

These words had weight. The woman spoke simply but with absolute conviction. The room pulsed with expectancy. Edward Lepage went completely still. He relaxed his grip on the child, which in turn allayed it's crying. His face fell blank, as though not wanting to betray the fear that quite obviously coursed within him. He averted his gaze away and cleared his throat.

"Mallie is still not a name recognised by the Church. It is an aberration of Mary, a colloquialism. It would be blasphemous to call the child so."

"Call yon pup Mary then, in this church. Those that love her will know her as Mallie. Those that matter. On with it then, we've a birthing to tend over in Grindleton."

Despite his warnings, the Minister baptised the child 'Mary 'Repentance' Device', because Presbyterians are known to be egregious. Yet it didn't matter, as he died the following spring from a sudden apoplexy and nobody missed him very much.

A Cunning Woman

"Wait on me, Dary Nabb, or may God drop his clog on thee!"

A disembodied voice disturbed the gloomy solitude of the dell with the cutting clarity of a Whitsun bell. Its owner presently came into view as she clambered gracelessly down a bracken sodden slope, entering the quiet hush of the wood whose stunted sickly trees seemed to silently regard her for a moment.

The girl was little more than fifteen, just a year younger than her mother had been when she faced down Lepage all those years ago. Despite her youth she was solidly built, as though her young body was already acquainted with hard labour. She wore an exquisite rag of a dress, inherited from her intrepid mother. It would once have been magenta but was now a faded russet and the fine fabric was now tattered and torn along the hem. She did own simple, brown dresses like the other lasses in the village, but she had wanted to impress Dary with her fanciest dress today. It made her feel as fearless as her mother had been, before she had been lost to the Blue Sickness.

The dress was now heavily hemmed in mud from the girls exploits over The Hill, playing at kiss chase with Dary Nabb, the tanners son. Despite her strangely elegant dress, her leather boots were audaciously robust and made light work of the twisted roots between the trees. Mallie Device owned a simple, round face which often carried a sweet smile for those she loved. However, it could just as soon turn sour upon those she disliked. Youth made her innocent face err on the cusp of pretty, although time and the rough life destined for her would quickly take their toll and it would soon grow hard. A curl, the fiery colour of autumn, had escaped the braid which encircled her head. She batted it away distractedly. Mallie followed her quarry through the dell, feigning annoyance at Dary, for she truly enjoyed the sport of chasing him. Truth be told, she took delight in most things Dary did.

Creeping between two gnarled and ancient yews, the girl spied her prey. She tip-toed behind him, leaned in and deftly swiped the cap from his head, letting his blonde curls spill forth over his eyes. He cried out in mock outrage and turned round to snatch it back.

"Mallie, you little besom! I shall tell Owd Mother Fortune of you and I shan't be sorry when she turns you into a sack of corn!"

Mallie laughed and her eyes sparkled mischievously.

"Ha! You know Owd Mother would sooner turn herself into a sack of corn than hurt a hair on Mallie's head. Her loves me best."

The pair chased each other around the trunk of a diseased looking elm, Mallie giggling, her sweetheart Dary calling her a wicked baggage. So absorbed were they in their flirtation they failed to realise that they were being observed. A subtle shift in the atmosphere of this lonely place gradually drew the couple's attention. Dary took his cap back from Mallie's unresisting hands and jammed his unruly hair back underneath it, all the while scanning the wood for what, he did not know.

"Don't be afeared, Dary, tis just th'owd wood. You're safe with me," she reassured him.

Dary shot her a look back. She knew she had spoiled the mood now. He always hated it when he had to acquiesce to that singular knowledge and craft of her infamous family. For Mallie was a Device. A generation of Device's had been lost in Pendle, taken to the Castle City and their necks broken for harm to man by witchcraft. Mallie's own great-grandmother, 'Owd Mother Fortune' was Demdike's niece, she who had been queen witch of Pendle; second only to the devil himself it was said.

Owd Mother Fortune's granddaughter had committed the sin of bearing Mallie out of wedlock, to the son of a local squire. The boy swiftly regretted fraternising with witches, no matter how pretty they seemed. For fear and shame of the Device name, the unwilling father promptly took the King's Shilling and was spirited away to war, never to be seen again. And so the cycle continued. Whispers of their crimes, their deviousness, their craft still filled the villages of Pendle, even after all these years. And even though the Witchfinders had long abandoned Pendle, it was said the devil still walked wild in the county.

"We shouldn't have come here, Mal."

Dary was still looking uneasy. Mallie looked around, using the skills passed down to her by her strange family and her natural instincts to sniff out the danger. Yes, perhaps they shouldn't have dared come here, but their foolish games had bled them of sense and so here they now stood. Here. Of all places. The Witch Wood of Pendle.

"It's just a boggarty tale, there's no truth in it, don't be scared. You know who we are, you know the truth, even when others still talk. That's why you're so dear to me, Dary Nabb." Mallie graced him with a warm, loving smile. Dary smiled bravely back and took the girls hand. She thrilled at his touch, but she had not been convinced by her own words. Something was wrong.

"You just wait till Mouldheels gets you! You won't be brave then, you'll come crying for your Dary!" said the boy, and with that he nipped her at the soft flesh in the crook of her elbow. Forgetting her worries momentarily, the girl squealed in glee.

At this, there came a loud scoffing from the dark canopy above that felled them to sudden silence. Dary did the unthinkable, and lifted his gaze to the heavens. There was a girl in the elm tree, sitting in a position that afforded her a full, unadulterated view of his childish antics. He suddenly felt absolutely foolish. He subconsciously took a step away from Mallie and peered upward curiously at the stranger in the tree. She really was very pretty, even from her perch in the boughs. She smiled down at him with a look of utter scorn that he could barely comprehend, and began a dainty descent. Mallie looked from the strange girl to Dary and saw that his broad, handsome face was enchanted. She looked back at the girl. Hmm, perhaps enchanted was the right word.

When on the ground the girl walked smartly up to them, curtsied neatly and introduced herself.

"I'm Elizabeth."

Mallie narrowed her eyes. The girl was the most curious creature either of them had ever seen. Her dark mop of hair was completely unbraided and untamed. It flowed wildly down her shoulders in a dark wave to the small of her back and seemed to contain all manner of leaves, twigs, old beads and goodness knows what else. Her eyes were also extraordinarily dark, almost black, looking pupiless in certain lights. Her small face was made prettily indeed, with fine almond eyes and a sweet snub of a nose. Her little bud of a mouth was alarmingly crimson against the stark white of her face. Her dress seemed woven from the forest floor itself, a multitude of browns and oranges, covered in leaf litter. Around her narrow shoulders she clutched a woollen shawl of darkest claret. She looked at them hungrily. Dary bowed and then, somewhat impulsively, took her small white hand and kissed it.

Mallie stepped between them and shattered the genteel reverence with her own rough manners.

"You're not from Pendle," she stated, suspiciously.

"No," said the girl smiling. "Not anymore."

"How's that then?"

"I'm from over Amounderness way. My people stay in Bispham-cum-Norbreck now but we once had...roots...in Pendle." The girl sounded almost wistful.

"What brings you here?"

"My Aunt is sick. I am sent with a cure for her malady."

"What ails her?"

"The grippe."

"Hmm." Mallie could feel in her bones that something was not right about this stranger.

"What cure do you bring?"

The girl smiled knowingly.

"Oysters."

Dary smiled back at the girl as though they shared some private joke. Mallie was swiftly losing her patience. And she didn't like the way Dary looked at the girl.

"Do you make a habit of spying on people in Bispham-cum Nowhere?"

"Mallie! Remember yourself!" Dary exclaimed, mortified by her rudeness.

"I am remembering myself Dary Nabb – you'd do well to remember yourself too!"

Dary looked down, chastened, hurt, embarrassed. Elizabeth grinned as though she was thoroughly enjoying his anguish. Mallie regretted snapping at Dary but he had spoken out of turn. She did not suffer fools. Even when she loved them.

Mallie walked away from them both whilst she considered her next move. She was torn between doing what had been taught to her – helping those in want of it, and leaving the interloper unsupervised. She fought with the decision momentarily, cursed under her breath and turned her attention back to the girl.

"Oysters won't shift her grippe for long. You want whimberries for that. Stay here, I know where they grow."

And with that, because it was in her nature to help and to heal, Mallie Device disappeared, back up the slope at the foot of the great hill of Pendle.

Elizabeth watched her leave impassively before turning to regard Dary coldly until he met her gaze again. She raised an eyebrow archly in query.

"Pay no mind to Mallie, she doesn't know no better."

"And you do, do you...Dary Nabb?" The odd girl said his name liked she owned it.

"Aye, I do!" he protested, put out.

"Is that so?"

The girl called Elizabeth walked around him slowly, as if assessing him like a pig at market, brazenly and without propriety. Dary shifted uncomfortably.

"Tell me, why does this dreary little place have you as scared as a goose at Christmas?"

Dary swallowed and considered her question for a moment. He leaned in, conspiratorially.

"Because this is Witch Country."

At this the girl threw her head back suddenly and let out an ugly and alarming cackle.

Up on the slope, stooped over a patch of purple moorland berries, Mallie abruptly cried out as though she had been pricked with a pin. She shot upright, her body tensed and she sniffed the air once. She winced again in pain, as though something powerful was blocking her from looking at it, even in the safety of her own head. She dropped the foraged whimberries and took flight down the hill to the dark wood beneath. Her heavy boots thudded on the damp ground, kicking up clods of earth, freckling her face with mud.

She broke through into the thicket where she had foolishly left her beloved with the stranger from the coast. Dary stood by the stranger's side, his face vacant and grey. The girl smiled widely, showing irregular teeth the colour of treacle. She took Dary's large, rough hand and bent his long fingers back effortlessly, one by one, snapping the bones, twisting the knuckles sickeningly. Dary did not scream out. Somehow that was worse.

Looking on in horror, Mallie screamed and lunged at the girl wildly in an effort to free him. With a flick of the girls hand Mallie was thrown bodily into the trunk of a tree with a force much greater than she had ever encountered. She hacked and coughed Winded, she led splayed awkwardly amongst the roots.

The girl gave one last twist and off came one of Dary's fingers. He fell to the cold earth and was motionless. The creature began to suck heartily on the finger, making disgusting slurping sounds. She was sucking the marrow from the bone. Sucking the very marrow whilst Dary still lived on.

"Ahh the finger-bone of a Pendle lad, I have missed that!"

"NO!" cried Mallie, in disgust and dismay.

"Quiet, little witch girl. Go play with your berries, you're no match for me."

The girl began to chew, splintering the bone with her blackened teeth. Mallie retched and reeled, almost swooned, at the repulsive scene. She caught herself. She needed to be strong for Dary. Perhaps she could save him yet.

"Not real. You're not real. Cunning folk like me an' me mam, an' th'Owd Mother, we're real. People call us witches because we birth the babbies, we heal the ailing an' sick. An' we care for the dying. But witches like you, devils...you're not real!" Mallie yelled, breathlessly.

"Oh, I'm not the devil. But he does send his regards." She dropped the finger-bone and walked over to her.

"And I assure you, I am very real. In fact, the last time I walked abroad in Pendle the fun I had caused many a broken neck. Poor things." The witch grinned evilly.

"But you're just a child!"

"Am I?" said the thing, as it closed the space between them.

Mallie Device, acting now on impulse alone, delivered a swift boot to the witch's stomach, which caught her off-guard. She then attacked fearlessly, dragging her nails down the creature's cheeks, driving her fingers into its eyes, pulling at its matted hair, which was wick with lice and spiders. Outraged, the witch pulled away and drew her hands back, as if to deliver some devastating final blow to her attacker, when a booming and ancient voice filled the wood.

"You will not harm that child. None will ever harm that child whilst there is breath in my body."

A shriek and then there was silence.

The witch was gone.

The Wishing Stone
by Adele V Robinson

I was nineteen and about to make promises as Godmother to my sister's first child. A clear winter day surrounded the picturesque church in the Lancashire village of Woodplumpton, its pews tightly packed with well-wishers from both my own and my brother-in-law's family. The vicar brimmed with enthusiasm as he conducted the ceremony, its formalities completed with the wetting of the baby's head. He then began to tell us a little about the history of the church, and the story of a local witch.

Meg Shelton had lived in the village where it was said she did many wicked things. When she died, Meg was buried in the churchyard despite her reputation as a witch. The vicar said she managed to claw her way out to commit more terrible acts until the villagers finally captured the 'resurrected witch'. This time, they buried her in a deep, narrow, grave head down and put a huge boulder on top so that she couldn't dig her way out again.

Surprisingly for a man of faith, the vicar told us all that if we were to stand on top of the stone and turn three times anti-clockwise, Meg Shelton would grant us a wish. As we all emerged from the church, people were chatting and making a fuss of the baby, so I slipped away along the pathway to find the stone. It loomed large and was worn smooth with age with a small metal sign bearing her name.

I still have no idea why I stood on the stone and turned three times anti-clockwise, but I do remember what I wished for. Being full of joy I wished for everyone to be happy. Then I noticed the guests leaving the churchyard, so I gleefully ran over to my Dad and I linked his arm. He smiled at me and we walked towards the gate.

Suddenly something very cold touched the back of my neck and I shuddered. "Did someone walk over your grave?" Dad asked jokingly. I didn't reply but turned back to look towards the stone. A misty shape seemed to be hovering above it and I heard a strange voice whisper, "Will you help me to be happy again?" Dad tugged on my arm, "Come on dreamer, we will be late for the party." As we walked away, I looked back and the mist was gone.

A couple of nights later I awoke in the early hours. It was icy cold and I was suddenly aware of a small figure in a white dress standing at the bottom of my bed, beckoning to me. I felt compelled to run but then realised my body was actually levitating some two feet above the bed. Somehow I rolled over and came down on my feet, then ran to the bedroom door only to find it obscured by a pink satin curtain hanging on an old-fashioned metal runner. A strong smell of flowers invaded my nostrils and I turned to see an old worn bedspread and a tiny window with no curtains. Wherever I was, it was no longer my bedroom.

In terror I pushed the curtain to one side, grabbed an old round, metal doorknob and escaped into a reassuringly familiar corridor. Not looking back, I raced to my parent's bedroom door and burst in. Startled, they both sat bolt upright, mother exclaiming "What's wrong?" My voice was trapped in my throat and she got out of bed, gripping my shoulders with consoling hands. Shuddering and crying, I finally blurted out, "In my room! Please help me, there is something in my room."

Dad leapt out of bed, switching on the lights and picking up a shoe as went to look. A few moments later he returned and laughed it off. "You were having a nightmare, no one is in your room." Mum put on her dressing gown and went downstairs to get me a drink, while I sat on her bed shivering and unable to move.

The next morning, I told her what I had seen, and she nodded as I related every detail. "It obviously frightened you darling," she said. "I think it was all that nonsense about the witch in the churchyard. You have such a vivid imagination and it obviously played on your mind. Just try to forget it."

Weeks passed without incident and I busied myself at college, gradually coming to believe the apparition as probably just a nightmare. On the first Sunday in November, my boyfriend said that he and two friends were going to Windermere to collect a speed boat they kept moored on the lake, and tow it back for winter in his garage. I decided to spend the day at my health club for a swim and a ten minute slot on the sunbed.

Locking the door, I undressed and lay down on the bed with its remote control in my hand. But as I activated the canopy to lower, the air around turned very cold. The hairs on the back of my neck stood up as I had an overwhelming feeling of being in a coffin, buried alive. A blinding flash swept across my eyes and I saw a vision of a red boat adrift. It was hit violently from behind by something white, sending it flying into the air and crashing on top of another vessel coloured blue, both smashing on impact.

The vision passed and I was back on the sunbed, though not for long. Quickly dressing, I grabbed my shoes and ran out. Passing the young man who had let me into the room, he called after me, "You've only been in there for a couple of minutes." But I was instinctively racing home.

"What's wrong," said Mum, "You look like you've seen a ghost."

"I think Steve has been in an accident" I gasped, grabbing the telephone and dialling his number with shaking hands to no reply. I told Mum what I had seen, and told Dad too.

Later that evening the phone rang and it was Steve. "Are you alright," I asked frantically.

"Yes of course, are you?"

"Where the hell have you been!"

"All right, calm down. It was such a beautiful day that we went out on the lake skiing, and I've just got back."

I breathed a sigh of relief, explaining "Sorry, thought you'd been in an accident," but refraining from telling him what I had seen.

"Well, we decided to leave the boat up there and fetch it next weekend. Perhaps you can come up with us."

The following Sunday came and I declined his invitation, convinced I had some kind of premonition and my going with him would cause the accident. Instead, I drove into Blackpool to help out with an exhibition at the Winter Gardens, which kept me occupied for the rest of the day. As evening fell I left the venue, backing out my red Ford Escort into a one-way street with cars parked along both sides. Then there was a blinding white flash.

Next thing I knew a fireman was banging on the passenger side window and opening the door. "You have to get out quickly love," he said, "It might set on fire." I was in shock and more concerned where my missing right shoe had got to. He reached into the car and pulled me towards him, then lifted me down to the ground. My car was on top of a metallic blue Allegro parked on the opposite side of the road, and I had been hit from behind by a huge, white Ford Granada estate. The real meaning of the vision slowly dawned as I watched the fire fighters fill my petrol tank with water.

Miraculously, there was not a scratch or bruise anywhere on my body. Dad came to fetch me, relieved to see that I was in one piece. As he drove us home I said, "Oh my God Dad, this is what I saw happen two weeks ago, only it was Steve not me. What does it mean?"

"You're just shaken up," he assured. "Try to relax. It will all be OK."

How could I relax with my life changed so suddenly? Why should I see an apparition in my bedroom? Why did a premonition of an accident involving Steve then happen to me? It seemed crazy and I needed to understand what was going on. Sleeping fitfully over the next few nights, I finally made an appointment to see my GP. She listened and issued a prescription for anti-depressants. I didn't cash it.

* * *

A few days later, Mum came into town with me and, as we walked towards the site of the accident, I noticed a small brick building bearing the sign Spiritualist Church and something hit me. "This is where I have to go Mum. They will be able to help," I said, not knowing why I said it.

The church notice listed an open service that afternoon and people were already gathering inside. Mum held my hand as we walked down the stairs into a bright room with chairs in a semi-circle and sat down. After a while a small, stocky woman came into the room with two others who sat as she remained at the front. She introduced herself as Ruth and welcomed everyone to the meeting, before asking us to close our eyes and saying a prayer I had never heard before.

Ruth was looking directly at me when my eyes opened, smiling as she spoke to one of her two companions, "Look at the beautiful face of that young girl." Suddenly all eyes were on me, but then her expression and voice changed. "I am sorry but we don't allow that in here."

I looked at Mum, "Is she talking to me?"

"Yes I am talking to you," Ruth said angrily, "You can't do that in here."

"I'm not doing anything."

Another woman commented, "I don't think she realises that she is wide open." She then turned to me, "Is it your first time here love?"

"Yes, I haven't been here before."

Ruth smiled at me again. "Ah, that is alright. I will speak to you shortly".

Her attention turned to others and she began to give them messages. I listened quietly for a while, and then felt a shiver come on as everything in the room began swimming. The sensation turned into that of suffocation and I leapt out my chair, bolting towards the stairs.

"You need our help! You can't deal with it alone," one of the women called out as I ran.

"It's OK", I heard Ruth say. "She'll come back."

Mum found me outside, doubled over and panting for breath. She put a consoling arm around me. "What happened in there?"

"I don't know, Mum, but she's right, I have to go back inside. I need help to stop whatever is happening to me".

We remained outside until most of the people had left, then went back down the stairs where one of the two women was pointedly waiting. She walked over to a door and knocked, announcing "The young lady is here now." Mum and I sat as Ruth emerged and brought a chair over to sit directly in front of me. She then took my hands. "Now then child, let me see what I can do to help you." I wanted to speak, to tell her everything that had happened. But it was all so mixed up, I didn't know where to start.

Ruth spoke again. "You are walking around fully opened to any spirit that wants to enter."

"What? What do you mean?"

"When you came into the meeting earlier, someone was with you. A woman in a long white dress followed behind. She has long, black hair and is not of this time. She died a very long time ago. Do you know who she might be?"

"I am not sure. I have seen a woman like that, at the end of my bed in the middle of the night. Very strange things have been happening to me ever since."

"It is your attention she wants. She came to you for help. Who do you think she might be?"

It sounded ridiculous to me but I told her about the Christening and the stone on the grave belonging in Meg Shelton.

"Did you make a wish?" Ruth asked.

"Yes," I said, "I wished for everyone to be happy. Then I had a car accident, which I realised I had foreseen but not happening to me. It doesn't make sense. Does she want to hurt me? Is she trying to kill me?"

Ruth stroked my hand, "We won't let her hurt you. You have connected with a troubled spirit and there is no doubt in my mind as to who it is. We need to find out what she wants so then we can put her to rest. But I will need to do some consulting first. Could you both come to my house this Saturday evening?" I nodded and she gave me her card.

* * *

Dad drove Mum and me to Ruth's house on Saturday after dinner. It was dark when we arrived in the small village and we located the whitewashed cottage at the end of a long narrow lane. He went to the village pub for a beer, saying he would come for us in an hour. I rang the doorbell, my heart thumping in anticipation as I waited for it to open. The other two ladies were both in the front room as Ruth ushered us in, where a circular table and five chairs were waiting in the centre. The dark green velvet curtains were closed and several candles stood lit on the mantelpiece while others flickered on tall stands behind the chairs.

Ruth sat at the far side and opened her arms. "Please sit down ladies." As we settled she asked us all to join hands then spoke in a monotone voice. "We call upon the spirit of Meg Shelton to come among us. Are you here Meg Shelton? Please speak to us."

An icy chill filled the room and I looked around to see if a window was open. Several of the candles blew out, plunging the room into a deepening gloom. Ruth's appearance seemed to change. She looked gaunt and seemed to be surrounded by a mist. I closed my eyes and when I opened them, the woman was standing next to Ruth, her long black hair blown back from her face by a freezing cold wind.

I felt my Mum squeeze my hand tightly as the apparition opened its mouth and let out a piercing scream. Then in a deep unearthly voice it cried, "They buried me alive. They said I was evil. They said I was a witch like them as came from Pendle Hill. I didn't deserve what they did to me. I am not a witch. Tell them I am not a witch." Ruth's head dropped onto the table with a bump and the apparition was gone.

I let out a long sigh. One of the others stood up and poured some glasses of brandy, handing one first to Ruth and then to each of us. Mum knocked hers back, visibly shaken, but I felt relief in the realisation of what the spirit wanted of me. She wanted me to know.

So next day I went to the library and started my research. Over the following weeks, I discovered that Meg Shelton was born in the village of Singleton and had moved to a small cottage in Woodplumpton, one of several that belonged to the local Lord. No one in the village knew her or knew why she was there. They didn't take well to strangers.

Not long after she arrived, a local farmer reported that some of his cows' milk had been stolen. As Mistress Shelton lived alone and did no work, the finger of suspicion fell on her. Rumours began to circulate that a man in black, who must be the devil, was seen through an upstairs window in the dead of night. People said that she shape-shifted, often taking the guise of a wild animal prowling the village at night. She was an outsider and was labelled 'the Fylde hag'.

The fact is her real name was Margery Hilton and came to Woodplumpton to have the baby of her lover, who was married. After her son was born, he was taken from her to the manor house and raised as the legitimate child of the Lord and his wife. She later died in a terrible accident when crushed by a barrel in the passageway at the side of her cottage, the tragic circumstance of which was rather too convenient. Meg had no need of a barrel.

She was buried in consecrated ground but was not dead. Waking, she fought to claw her way out of the suffocating grave and escaped. It was venom and superstition that drove the villagers to bury her alive for a second time. Head down, with a huge boulder instead of a gravestone, they sealed her fate and damned her soul to wander for eternity.

Then I came along and made a wish that tied me to her. I wished for everyone to be happy, and everyone included Meg Shelton. So I wrote her story and submitted it to the county newspaper for all to know, and the power of the press did the rest.

Flowers are often placed on that stone in Woodplumpton churchyard. Now it is the grave of Margery Hilton, formerly of Singleton, who died in tragic circumstances, hundreds of years ago. She who finally rests in the knowledge her truth is told and name cleared.

Let her hang!
by Bridget Kenny

Boiling bubbles and eyes of frog
You would think that is what I say
When in reality
Thing's just don't work that way.

Earth, fire, water and air
The blessings we are given
My Gods-
My prayer.

Captured in 1612
My future in their hands
People who never understood
Why I was really dancing in the woods.

My hooded eyes could only
Vaguely see
The torture and hate that
Was about to be inflicted on to me.

My trapped wrists,
Hands covered in my blood
This pain is something
I have never understood.

Scattered voices,
I could barely hear
Pacing back and fourth
Sometimes moving near.

Chants going around
And around my mind
But the words to speak aloud-
These, I could not find.

The hood was pulled off
So roughly
The light was blinding
My eyes! I could not see.

My mouth forced open
What next could be?
I felt the pain, blood gushing.
It flooded out if me.

A while went by, blood still dripped
From the place
Where my tongue was
From my mouth, ripped.

This place- my home
Where I lay my head
Surrounded by people
Shouting, celebrating 'the witch is dead!!'

It is fascinating to see
The torture they had put on to me
A shame, almost, that only I knew
The things these people will now be put
through.

From the moment my body went still
After hanging in the air
All standing around waiting
People from far and near.

One by one, they disappear
In gradual moments of attack
One looks in the mirror and whispers quietly
'Oh no, the witch is back!!'

In Which Way Shall I Die
By Barra Bromley

Beth and Kate weren't ready for death. At twenty-two, they linked arms against the world and laughed at their own invincibility. And despite living in a dull and dreary seaside town, salted with winter decay, they considered it an unworthy subject with which to fill their heads. Dying was for the old and the deserving. Yet following the screening of the latest film in the Lytham St Annes Fright Season, something changed.

It had to be said that the main protagonist in *One Hundred Ways to Die* looked uncannily like Kate, and Beth was to later reason this was why her friend had been so affected. There could be no other explanation. The dread implanted in Kate was not that one day she would die, but in *which* way it would happen. What awful method would be her lot? The options were so numerous, and all equally terrifying. Who could even wish them on their worst enemy?

Beth managed to stay grounded throughout Kate's unrest, but only because somebody had to. "It was just a film," she advised Kate at every opportunity. "Pure fiction and nothing more. You probably won't die for another sixty years, so why freak now?"

Kate found it hard to explain, and when she tried the blood drained from her cheeks. "Because..." she would start, "...because it's going to come round soon enough. Maybe sooner than sixty years... *very* soon, even. Who's to say? And what if I'm like that girl in the film, put in my coffin alive with no one knowing? What if I wear my fingers to the bone scratching to get out?"

"Then go for cremation, you crazy woman."

"That would be worse. Imagine burning to death like a shrimp on a hotplate..."

This would go on until Kate found another bone to worry, another method of dying to feast her fears upon. "What if I was to slowly suffocate with an intruder's hand across my face? Imagine how long it would take...My eyes could even pop out first and what then?"

With something amounting to patience, Beth would smile. "Statistically, that's highly unlikely. Your parents' house is more secure than the Queen's knickers."

Kate would listen yet she refused to hear. "It could happen out on the street, a stranger waiting in a dark alley?"

"Keep out of dark alleys, then!" said Beth, cursing the day they had gone to see the film. Where was Kate's usual interest in flirting, and shoes, and other girlish mayhem? Shouldn't they be hunting down boyfriends, or dancing till the wee hours in some prohibitively expensive nightclub? Clearly nothing would ever be so free and innocent again, or as much fun. All because of someone's badly written script, woven in with grisly scenes that happened to be set in a seaside resort. Though no one could deny it looked uncannily like Lytham St Annes...

Things grew worse over time. After a fairly chilled Sunday, watching laughably bad videos from the 80s, Kate had an idea. She would take the family dog for a walk along the sea front. Maybe with courage she could rediscover her old self. "Hope you understand," she said as she saw Beth to the door. Yet as she led Foxy along the darkening promenade she shivered. Rather than lose the enveloping paranoia that threatened her sanity, she felt it grow in the damp, cloying atmosphere. She watched as a sea fret edged its way inland. Soon it would be difficult to differentiate one shape from another...

When she reached the busiest part of the seafront, where fairy lights attempted to pierce the gloom, Kate's fear increased. She began to dwell on a particular scene from *One Hundred Ways to Die*. The film's main protagonist (and Kate's doppelganger) walked a similar stretch of seafront where a dark and gloopy beast slithered from the confines of a beached ship. It went on to consume not only the film's main character, but several passersby. Not a nice thing to witness, however fictional.

Fortunately there were no resting vessels along this part of the coast. But there was the old deckchair hut, faintly silhouetted against the sketchy moon. Kate pondered if it was as innocent as it appears. Perhaps it was home to a creature with an insatiable appetite.

For a brief moment Kate sat on a bench and submitted to the image. She closed her eyes and envisaged her breath stolen by a great ball of slime, and no one to hear her final cries. How long would the process take? What would it feel like to die with a membrane of jelly against her face, tight as cling-film around a ham?

This bowing to her morbid and overactive imagination soon wore Kate down. She endlessly replayed the many ways to die, each with its own pain, its own isolation. Even dying of old age seemed unthinkable. If friends and family had already passed on then who would escort her into the night?

When they next met, Beth was shocked by Kate's agitated behaviour. Her time alone had made her worse, not better. Now Kate's hands seemed to have a life of their own, and her eyes hopped like flies in a jam jar. "We need to get away," Beth suggested, though more for her own sake. Madness and negativity were easy; it was sanity and positivity that required the uphill climb. What had Shakespeare said about treading the primrose path to the everlasting bonfire...?

Kate nodded in agreement, while appearing to listen to something unseen. "If you can arrange it..." she said, looking over her shoulder. But she had made up her mind. She would go along with anything Beth suggested for what other option did she have? It seemed Death was the one adversary from which there was to be no escape.

As luck would have it, Beth's aunt had a house close to the village of Barley which stood empty for the best part of each winter. They could retreat there and enjoy the peace of the countryside. "We can take walks across the moors," said Beth. "Maybe even learn about the local wildlife." She offered these suggestions convinced the change would break Kate's cycle of fear, but, as they approached the property, her friend reacted with terror. It could have been the figment of a horror writer's imagination with its neo-gothic façade, arched windows and mysterious turret. She had expected something modest but the house was the largest for miles around, and perhaps the most neglected.

The interior décor was plain and uninspired, though its ordinariness did not deter Kate from starting a vigil at the living room window. She could not help but stare at the gloomy hillside just beyond the fields, something about its shadowy mass filling her with premonitory dread. When Beth told Kate the name of the hill her reaction was immediate. "What do you mean, *Pendle* Hill? You mean the actual place that's connected with those awful witches?"

"That is pure myth," said Beth as she set a tray down on the coffee table. "Based on silly superstitions. Anyway, come and drink your coffee. I can't believe how much money my aunt spends on these chocolate biscuits..."

Kate was not so easily lured off topic. "You never mentioned your aunt's connection with this area before. Isn't there meant to be some force up on Pendle that makes people feel kind of weird, sort of angry and stuff?"

Beth suddenly felt an overwhelming need for alcohol. "Get a grip, hon," she said with a silent tut. "Only stupid people believe that kind of nonsense, not people like you, with your degree in Philosophy. Come on, let's forget the coffee and give the village locals the benefit of our company."

Kate turned away from the window. "Great," she said without conviction. "I'll get my purse." She made her way up to the landing, finding it in hushed stillness, as if waiting for someone to join it. She hurried past the open doors of the five bedrooms to the little boxroom which Beth thought she would prefer. Of course this wasn't the case. Though small, it was anything but cosy and seemed to embody everything she feared.

For a start, the room was rife with potential dying methods, all of them terrible. There was the thick cord around the waist of the dressing gown, hanging from a hook on the door and perfect for twisting around a young, fragile neck. Then there was the heavy wardrobe with its ormolu mouldings, waiting to be toppled. As for the bedside table, there was nothing sensible like a lamp on it. Instead, an arrangement of jars filled with this and that, all stuff that could be rammed down her throat by a malicious stranger. And god knows what wicked vibes lay embedded inside the nearby hill. *Pendle* Hill. Perhaps they were even wending their way toward the house this very moment...

Kate could have gone on naming potential death traps or reeling off horror tropes, but was interrupted by her friend, impatient for a pint. "Come on, pain," said Beth with the strained bonhomie of a Girl Guide leader. "Let's get moving."

Their pub crawl was somewhat shortened by the fact the village boasted only two pubs of note. Though there were four places of worship, each a behemoth against the darkening sky. "Bloody typical," Beth commented. "For each place you drink yourself silly, there are two to drown you in guilt!" She laughed at her own joke and Kate joined in, giving the impression she was beginning to relax. But impressions can be deceiving...

On their way to the second pub, Kate noticed a cavernous hole in the road. As Beth chatted about what they could do the next day, Kate wondered how it would be to fall into such a pit, to hear your legs snap, or have a discarded metal spike insert its way into your spine? Worse, how would it feel to scream and scream and remain unheard?

By bedtime, Kate was actually glad to be away from her friend. Beth no longer understood her fears, she could tell. On their return to the house Beth took herself off to the kitchen to make a sandwich, not even asking if she was hungry too. Now Kate sat alone in her room, its cell-like proportions giving full rein to her worries. What if instead of a maniac, it was a ghost that crept upon her in the night? Maybe poisoned by some witchlike crone who peddled in deadly herbs? Such fatalities were easy to imagine in a decrepit old place like this.

Kate's morbid line of thinking found itself accompanied by a faint tap-tap-tap in the underbelly of the house, and her imagination fired up on cue. The house may be incapable of keeping anything out and there had been stories about wild animals on the prowl, zoos apparently incapable of keeping its inmates in order. Who knew what was out there? The house could be in cahoots with Pendle Hill, absorbing the landscape's nasty history into its fabric.

Kate felt dizzy, possibly the effects of the beer. If anything *did* happen, who was there to hear? Earlier, when she had groaned at the rural isolation of the location, Beth had reluctantly admitted that yes, it *was* a house where things could happen. She had then gone strangely silent.

After taking a deep breath, Kate switched the overhead light off and ran to bed. With pulled duvet pulled chin high and ears cocked, her own mind began taunting her again. Where was that breathing coming from, and why did it stop when she held her breath to listen? Then she realised it was her own and bravely told herself "Everything is fine, long as I don't need to use the loo during the night." That would mean creeping along that endless bloody landing, past the top of that horrible staircase…

The oppressiveness of the room weighed on her like a straightjacket. With the light switch by the door and out of immediate reach, the thought occurred of something hiding in the wardrobe and waiting for night to fall. Why had she forgotten to check the damn thing? But then came the very sound she had been dreading and this time knew was real. Footsteps, out on the landing…pad pad, pad…then silence.

She considered calling out for Beth, but knew this would irritate her further. She held her breath again and listened, eyes wild with fear. *Oh my God, was that the door knob being twisted?* A chill ran up her spine. So she was about to be haunted, for real, and her death would be at the gossamer hands of a spirit. Perhaps it was even the ghost of Demdike, the very worst of them…

Yet there was nothing as insubstantial as a ghost at her door, instead an all too corporeal crash as it flew back against the wall and a garish light streamed in from the landing. Kate raised her hands to protect her eyes and tried to gather sense from this unexpected turn in events, however there was no time for such a luxury. A heavy liquid anointed her with its rank smell and soaked the surrounding bed. She experienced a brief moment of recognition before being numbed by another unexpected twist.

"Did you seriously think I could have carried on with your constant whining?" The voice from the doorway spoke with careless and cruel venom, and the first tear of many dampened Kate's cheek. This real terror felt worse than all her recent imaginings put together. "Beth...?"

"How many sodding times have I tried to help you with your silly fears? But did you listen? Nope. You've just gone on and bloody on..."

Kate struggled to make sense of her friend's mood. Was it possible that Beth was still joshing about? She had always been the one with the jokes. "Don't be upset with me," said Kate with a placating smile. "You know I've never got the whole horror film thing, too sensitive I guess..."

Beth smiled but not in a way that Kate could understand. "The trouble, my friend, is that your sensitivity runs only one way. Have you ever considered how annoying you can be?"

Kate wanted to answer, but the way her friend held the lit match rendered her silent. Beth didn't smoke cigarettes and there were no candles in the house. Then, instinct finally guessed intention and propelled Kate to her feet, ready to spring from the bed. However, in the twist of a second, she was caught in a ring of fire. Attempting to roll beyond the curtain of flame, something bludgeoned her on the head and she fell onto her back, fenced in by hot, yet icily cold flames.

She could just make out Beth's outline, illuminated in the doorway like a crazed Okie in a slasher movie. Death at the hands of a friend was the one thing she hadn't considered. Her confusion gave way to the sheer hell of this knowledge, while searing pain inserted its way into her nerve endings. Flesh shrivelled, muscle shrank. The wheels of fortune now spun the room into a wicked, fiery dance of death.

"So, Kate," croaked Beth as she stepped back from the smoke. "Now you're experiencing what you feared most, eh? The lonely, agonising death you'd been dreading. And who's going to hear you, hmm? Or let's change that shall we? *I* can hear you screaming perfectly, but will I do anything about it? I don't think so."

Kate had an awareness that her friend talked on. There was a noise outside of the sizzling from within but what was being said? Her ears shrivelled back like burning cigarette paper and, around these ghastly stubs, her singed hair added to the stench of burnt meat. What was left of her physical self impulsively tried to jump from the bed once again, but she had become one with the bedding, the lumps of duvet and its floral cover stuck to her like medieval buboes. The last thing she saw before the flames licked her eyeballs was her raised arm, melting into the furnace that attacked with such relish.

"What did you say the other day, Kate? Imagine burning like a shrimp on a hotplate? Well now you know, girl...now you know."

And, indeed...now Kate did.

We are the Mist
by Petula Mitchell

We are the mist on Pendle Hill, the lingering clouds.
Taken from that lonely place and jeered at by the crowds.
We were hung, we swung, feared and reviled,
But we are not forgotten, history knows our tale.

So, what of our souls that wander earth forever?
Bodies buried at the crossroads, hidden in the heather.
Damned from heaven for we did the devils work.
Where shall we spend eternity, restless as we've been?

Look up to the hill top and see us there
Seeking out our accusers or failing that their kin.
So, beware when milk turns sour or fortune fails.
When sickness strikes and takes your young or frail

We are the whisper in the night time, the tolling of the bell.
We are your darkest nightmare, the harbingers of hell.
So when Pendle wears a misty shroud it isn't just the
weather.
It's the swirling of the murdered souls, residing there
forever.

Once Every Blood Moon
by Barry McCann

It is a melancholic night that has no stars yet presided by the fullest of moon. Looming huge and blood warm, the hunger moon watched down on the old earth below, spying on those who dared to be out in its presence. And there was one lost in its glare, attempting to negotiate the maze of the unfamiliar.

Stuart Dodgson drove along the circular road around Pendle Hill having been advised it was the shortest cut to Burnley. But the ever twisting narrow lane was endless, each turn a promise broken, until his headlights shone on the sign "Newchurch-in-Pendle."

Pulling up in the deserted hamlet, Stuart checked his written directions which advised taking the next right to Roughlee. Another moonlit sign pointed to Jinny Lane, and he duly steered his car on what proved to be another spiralling road plunged in darkness.

He was carefully taking a bend when the woman suddenly appeared, materialising in the glare of his headlights like a ghost. Stood in the middle of the road, she waved her hands to stop and he came to screeching halt. She ran over as he wound down the side window.

"Thanks for stopping. Sorry to have alarmed you."

"It's okay. Are you in trouble?"

The woman pointed over to a car parked just off the road.

"Broken down, think the gearbox has packed in. And I can't phone for help, there's no signal around here."

Stuart pulled out his mobile and checked. "No, none on mine either. I can give you a lift to the nearest village perhaps?"

"That would be great, though I'm concerned about my patient. She'll be worrying as to where I've got to."

"Patient?"

"Yes, I'm a doctor. Doctor June Brierley. I attend remote patients in their homes. Was on my way to an old lady in Blacko to give injections and stuff."

"Would you like me to drive you there first?"

"Oh, if you could that would be wonderful. I don't want to impose."

"Well, it sounds important."

"It is, else I wouldn't take advantage like this. Anyway, there's some gear I need to fetch from my car. Would you mind?"

He followed his new passenger over as she opened her boot and extracted an old fashioned looking Gladstone bag, placing it on the floor. She then produced a large plastic holdall and handed it to him, followed by a gas canister which he also took.

"What's that?"

"Oxygen, she has respiratory problems so I set up an oxygen tent. Ten minutes in that does her the power of good."

"Ten minutes?" His concern was not lost on her.

"Listen, I don't expect you to stay, just drop me off. She has a landline and I can phone the hospital to send transport. You're doing enough already."

Loading the gear into his car, the pair then set off, Dr. Brierley's instructions being to follow the signs to Blacko until she directed otherwise.

"Can't think of a worse place to break down," Stuart said by way of conversation. "And miles away from a signal."

"Not to mention Jinny Lane of all places," she lamented.

"Oh, what's special about Jinny Lane?"

"You won't find locals there at night, so I was relieved when you turned up."

"Are they scared of Pendle witches or something?"

"No, the Headless Horseman."

"The what?"

"Headless Horseman of Jinny Lane, another local legend. Wish I had a horse. At least they don't break down."

Stuart shook his head. "People in this day and age, believing nonsense like that?"

"Afraid so, folk round 'ere and all that," she said in a mock countryside accent. "Still, can't blame them really. Not after that killing a couple of years back. Enough to make anyone think twice about being out at night."

A bell began to ring in his mind. "Think I remember. Really grisly, wasn't it?"

"Young man from Burnley, found over a stone wall minus his head. Never found that."

"And they never got who did it?"

"No, but then they didn't last time."

"Last time?"

"Oh, yes, about twenty years ago. Woman vanished from her house in Sabden and turned up near the reservoir, again missing her you-know-what. Locals reckon it's the Jinny Lane horseman."

With that thought, she reached into her coat and produced a tubular packet. "Fancy a mint?"

"I'm fine, thanks."

She playfully nudged him with her elbow. "Go on, they're sugar free."

"Okay, thanks." He took a sweet and inserted it into his mouth, as she did the same and began to suck it quite pronouncedly.

With Pendle Hill behind them, Dr. Brierley pointed up to a turret silhouetted from behind by the deeply reddish moon.

"Blacko Tower," she announced, slurping her mint. "Looks great highlighted like that. Blood moons are so rare."

"It's huge, must be a close orbit."

"Come visiting you might say... Oh, take a right at the next crossroads."

Doing as instructed, Stuart's car accelerated up gradient and it was not long before he was told "The house is just off on the left. You can pull into the driveway."

Stuart turned through an open gate and halted just outside the house. There was no light on, and no sign of life.

"You sure she's home?"

"Has to be, she's housebound. Could you help bring my things in?"

"Yes, of course."

The pair got out and unloaded, Stuart carrying the holdall and canister as before. Dr. Brierley rang the front door bell and briefly waited. With no answer forthcoming, she produced a key and unlocked it.

Entering a dark room, she switched on a light to reveal a settee and chairs with a staircase by the side. She shouted "Mrs. Southworth?" only to be greeted by silence. Placing her bag on the coffee table, she instructed Stuart "Put that lot on the floor. I'll check upstairs, probably in bed."

As Dr. Brierley ran up the staircase, Stuart's curiosity took him to the kitchen. Flicking on the light, it was quite modern for a seemingly old house. His eyes blurred for a moment as he felt a dizziness suddenly come on. It passed just as quickly and he then noticed the back door slightly ajar. Walking over to pull it open, he looked out to see nothing but darkened fields.

Dr. Brierley ran in behind him with panic in her voice. "She's not here!"

"This door was open, but can't see anyone outside."

"She wouldn't go outside. She's too insecure about stepping out the house alone."

"A visitor perhaps? Taken her out?"

"At night? Up here! Besides, she doesn't get many…Oh, shit!" Cutting herself short, she marched past Stuart to the open door and looked at the night sky. She then turned back to him, eyes burning with bewilderment and horror. "Oh, holy Christ!"

"What is it?"

"I just remembered something. Those two murders we talked about? There was another factor that linked them." She stepped closer to him. "They both happened around a blood moon. Another detail the locals whisper of."

"What you saying?"

"Don't you see? She's been taken! We'd better phone the police."

Stuart nodded. "Where is it?"

"By the front door where we came in, I'll check out back, just in case."

He found the phone on its own small table and picked up the receiver. After tapping it a few times, he shouted "Dr. Brierley? It's dead!"

By the time she got there, he had found the line wrenched from the junction box. "It's been cut off deliberately."

"No doubt to slow us down. Probably saw us coming, which means they left in a hurry."

"No one passed us on the lane so they must have gone in the other direction. I'll get in the car and try catching them up. You stay here and I'll send the police as soon as I can."

"Wait!" She grabbed him by the hand. "You can't go after them on your own, it could be dangerous."

"I'll be careful, I promise."

Pulling his hand away, Stuart turned and went to open the front door. Suddenly he fell forward, catching and supporting himself on its handle.

"Are you all right?"

"Don't know..." His face was ashen and speech slurred. "Just had a turn. Legs feel weird."

"Come on." She pulled his arm over her shoulders and helped him over to the couch, gently setting him down.

"There you go, relax. How are you now?"

"Strange. My skin is tingling all over."

"Pins and needles?"

"Yes... Look, key's in my pocket, take the car, get help."

She shook her head. "I have to make sure you're okay first, then I'll find the next house and use their phone."

She took his wrist and felt for a few moments. "Your pulse is a tad slow. Are you on any medication?"

"No."

"Blood pressure problems?"

"Erm... normal, I think."

"Probably dropped suddenly, hence your faint. I'll take a reading in a minute, but first..."

She fetched her bag and extracted a small torch pen, shining it into each eye in turn. "Pupils pretty dilated. How's your skin feeling now?"

"Numb."

"Try wriggling your fingers."

He struggled to move them and she concluded "Muscles feeling tight?"

"Yes," his failing voice affirmed.

"Good, it's working then."

"...What?"

She patted his hand reassuringly and produced the tube of sweets from her jacket pocket. Taking another one, she sucked on it while explaining "The compound in the mint I gave you. At least the paralysis means you won't feel any pain."

His strangulated facial muscles managed to express bewilderment.

"As I said, tonight is the blood moon, and blood demands blood. You see, they got it wrong about the headless horseman." She stood up, affirming "I was a headless horsewoman, until the night Anne Whittle summoned me and offered to broker a pact with the lady moon." She gently brushed her fingertips down the sides of her face. "So in return for this, I send an offering when my lady breathes red. And tonight that honour is yours."

She reached into the bag and produced a surgical cleaver, its razor edge gleaming like a shining star. Holding it up as a looking glass, she admired her reflection in the gleaming metal and preened her hair, confessing "You know, I can never get enough of it." Pursing her lips, she looked back at Stuart and winked. "Well, all those centuries not having one."

Smiling, she crouched down and her other hand reassuringly gripped on his. "Please understand this is nothing personal, I have to choose my offerings at random." Tapping his hand again, she whispered "Muddies the waters, you see."

Later that evening, local police received frantic reports from Newchurch of a weather balloon gliding above the rooftops and towards the opulent moon. It was what hung from beneath that raised the alarm.

Roadside to Trawden Forest
by Alicia Cole

What I sought I found
each one gleaming
each one small, bright.
The roadside was still.
Just our silent place, together.
But he wouldn't sell
why, he never told
just held his sack.
I begged, I gripped my dress
perhaps he knew more than my face.
They're choice for healing
after all, pins, sorely needed.

It's true, I turned his heel
when he walked away,
felt the blood surge in me
like sap rising, heard him snap.
It's true, I smiled after
helped the old dotard up.
But the roadside is a tricky thing
the long, slow beat of it
the way the dirt settles.
Called to exultation
I stood beneath the sun's eaves
let good slip down like God.

I confessed to him later
so that I might hear
the constellations clear.
Confessed to him
my open mouth no longer dry dirt.
It was still where we were.
Our silent place, together.
Later, I went to the gallows
my head ringing free as loose hair.
Let my neck drop,
let light sing open
like the roadside's broad sway.

Ghosts in the Machine
by Janet Kenny

"Why do you have images of pins in different patterns as a screen saver?" Alison hovered over her colleague's shoulder as they both booted up their computers for the start of the working day.

"No idea, it was already on the PC when I started here. I've tried to change it but it keeps switching back to the same thing. Weird, eh?"

Alison gave a wry smile. "Mm, are you sure about that? Only I can assure you that there wasn't a problem with that PC before YOU started. I think that you've sabotaged it, to get Ian from IT up here so you can shake your ass for him, you tart. There isn't a day goes by without you two ogling each other."

"You're only jealous 'coz he fancies me and not you, Alison. He'll never fancy you, you're not his type."

The pair leaned in towards the screen, looking at it as if some voice or other form of communication would respond and answer their question.

"You know Alison, I get this feeling someone or something is watching me from within this machine. Sometimes I think I see a shadow in the screen when it's off, looks almost like a young woman with blonde hair."

"Tut don't be silly, there isn't even a webcam on these things, crikey they're still on Windows XP for God's sake."

They shrugged their shoulders, huffed and puffed at each other and carried on with office duties.

Alison, a sexy and a dominant female whom one would describe as 'blonde but dumb' pretended to tap away while glancing back at her colleague every few minutes. This was not the only thing Alison had begun to perceive, not since being bitten by her friend's black Labrador. Sometimes, it felt like she no longer fully retained her own identity, as if consumed by another being within her. One that occasionally strikes out both mentally and physically with urges of attacking the enemy in the next seat, to rid the desk of any female unlucky enough to sit there. It was neither through jealousy or envy that drove this scenario, just the same story turning like a wheel, time after time.

Then there were the nightmares she had been secretly nursing of late. There had been several nights where she half awakened in heaps of sweat, muttering olde and ancient cants while gripping the bed sheets to the point of tearing.

The night terrors did not so much haunt Alison as possess her. The cants were seemingly from some past era unknown to her, and had somehow wormed themselves into her unconscious mind. Because Alison had no conscious memory of where she may have learnt them, and could no longer recall their words once fully woken up. Consequently, she felt unable to discuss them, not that there was anyone she could think of to discuss them with. So, she kept cloaked behind a smiling veneer.

Every morning, she arrived at work early and seemingly happy, and remained good at her job. However, as she walked past the PC her colleague sat at, she paused each time with a sense that something or someone was watching from within her own self.

Since being bitten she also noticed that all her positive thoughts and energies repeatedly became dented, and a more vindictive and sinister side edged out. She took great pleasure in making each new person seated at that desk feel uncomfortable, usually with the tales of woe which she uncannily could recite without taking a breath.

She reached for her water bottle and drifted into a reverie, reliving the different scare tactics employed by her inner critical voice to rid the desk of any intruder. A sly smile became her, as she recalled all the tricks of olde magick used to scare previous colleagues. The inner voice described these methods to her and how to take advantage of any fear the victim feels, like a familiars whispering in her ear.

The best one to date had to be leaving an effigy on the desk for a newcomer called Amy. She tormented Amy relentlessly about witchcraft and paganism, pretending to be a High Priestess, and teased her about joining naked romps at Wicca ceremonies. After a few weeks, Alison brought in the wax effigy and explained how attaching pins and other personal stuff from a victim might affect their future.

She encouraged Amy to part with a few nail clippings and hair, and then securely bound them to the wax figure. Amy, young, gullible and in scepticism that such an idea could work, thought it funny and willingly gave Alison the required items for the spell.

According to the first aider, Amy became unwell and collapsed at her desk. While awaiting the ambulance, she suddenly came round with a start, and panic stricken. At first she gibbered incoherently, then leapt to her feet and ran with a possessed expression of terror on her face. Despite being pursued by her colleagues, she managed to run out of the building and straight into the road, not seeing the ambulance that was arriving for her. She was crushed against a wall as the driver unsuccessfully swerved to avoid her.

Luckily for Alison, no-one had noticed the effigy on the base of Amy's PC and she quickly hid it in her own desk drawer. Would anyone have guessed her guilt in having driven away another rival woman, only more permanent than intended this time?

The following morning, Alison arrived to find Amy's desk covered in flowers and sympathy messages. She added a small bunch of white lilies, carefully laying them on the empty chair and smiled mischievously. Any remaining feelings of guilt she had evaporated, making way for mischievous pleasure.

It had been several months since the tragedy and Alison still kept the wax effigy in her desk draw. It was now her totem of power and every recollection of what it did to Amy stirred that same feeling within her. Waiting for the others to go for their lunch break, she looked round to double check no one present was present and slid her hand into the drawer, stroking the hair and nails on the effigy inside. Aroused, her legs began to part, her lips became moist and breathing turned into panting.

"What the hell are you doing?" a voice yelled behind her. "Who on earth are you thinking of?"

Brought back to the real world, Alison instantly span round and glared at her colleague.

"I, I, I'm not sure, sorry I just drifted off somewhere." She pulled her hand from the drawer and slammed it shut, turning the key in its lock and withdrawing it. Standing up, she announced "I'm going to the canteen" and quickly departed.

She returned before lunch hour was over in the hope of having some time at the desk alone again. Sure enough, her colleague was absent and Alison sat, producing the key. She unlocked the top drawer and reached in for her beloved effigy, but felt nothing but a void and pulled the drawer fully open. To her horror, it had gone and a panic stricken hand covered her mouth.

At that moment the computer booted into life, seemingly of its own accord. A screen saver popped up, the image of the wax effigy with hair and nails attached by pins. She gasped and clutched her chest, looking around to ensure no one was there to see it. Frantically she typed on the keypad and tried to close the image but, like a frozen window, it stubbornly refused to go. She pressed escape, delete and finally the on/off button. The computer shut down but the graphic remained.

Instinctively, she touched the screen and felt strange, charged with energy despite the fact the power was off. Initially reasoning it to be static, her finger followed the outline of the image and sensed an electric pulse like a heart beating.

Her probing finger was suddenly brought to an involuntary halt and Alison realised the static was holding onto it. She tried to pull away, but the screen had somehow fused with her fingertip and, instead, it began drawing her body closer to the screen. On it, she began to see what appeared to be the outline of a young woman.

Alison mouthed at the image, "What do you want?" But there was no response. "Who are you?" Again, she was met with silence.

She tried to pull back in her chair but her finger was still ethereally attached to the screen. Reaching out with her other hand, she then hesitated to touch the computer. How could she explain both hands stuck to the screen and why unable to remove them?

She heard a clang and rustling as her colleague arrived back at the next desk and whispered to a squirming Alison "Good afternoon, how are you?"

"I've got superglue on the tip of my finger and I'm stuck on this wretched screen, any chance you could, like, try and prise me off it?" It was the best story she could think up in the circumstances."

"Prise you of it?" The colleague gave a puzzled frown.

"Or ask around for some acetate or something?" Her voice trailed off. She lowered her head in to the one palm still free and sighed, "Or even ask Ian?"

"You've not seen the signs since I've been working here, have you Alison?"

She jolted in her chair as the colleague bent forward, mouth level with her ear, and continued to whisper while stroking her arm.

"This is your punishment for being a constructive murderer, bullying everyone who sits at this desk, but you don't know why you're feeling possessed, do you?

Alison stammered, "How do you know that? I've never shared that feeling with anyone, honestly I.."

"Shut up you pathetic creature! When it's your turn, no one will feel your loss." He nodded at her screen. "This is the prelude to your turn... suicide they'll say. But we will both know that when the witch finder catches up, there's no escape from the online gallows."

"What are you talking about, it's just a virus from your PC to mine, it's jumped that's all."

"No, I don't think so, Alison. I've always known that you have seen Amy on the screen. She's a ghost in the machine, a malevolent one whose life ended because of you and your stupid curses."

The colleague pulled out Alison's effigy from his pocket, "You see, you belong to a long line of witches, except you didn't know." He stroked the doll, reminiscing "I stole Amy's nails and hair from it and recreated an entity on my home PC, before transferring onto a memory stick and bringing it here." He pointed to Alison's monitor. "I knew when the time was right, Amy would appear on your screen, and here she is my gorgeous granddaughter."

Alison eyes widened and her jaw dropped, and the male colleague tapped the screen.

"She admired you, you know. So I thought it fitting that you could look after her on the other side. This is why I started at this place, I too have my familiars, but they're not black cats or dogs, Alison. No this is the 21st century, mine are online and you are soon to join them."

"What do you mean? Familiars, what are you on about?"

He stroked Alison's hair, pulled up a chair and whispered.

"Sweet Alison, you and I are from a long line of rival families, feuding for years and it now has to stop. You are casting daemons on innocent folk. You the last of yours and me and Amy the last of mine. You, the last of the Devices, will lay to rest."

"Devices?" The name acted as incantation, prising open the sanctum in Alison's mind within which the secrets of her terrible dreams were kept. As they flooded out, she realised the meaning of his words as the history behind them were also recalled.

"But the other family were called Southern, but your name is John Lawson. Do you claim to be descended from them?"

"I speak not of that feud. I am descendant of John Law, the one your side cursed when he refused his pins. Well, to defeat one's enemy, learn their song. And your time has now come, Angel, to end this cursed misery."

Alison began to scream as John Lawson pushed her head against the screen, but it was too short lived for anyone to hear. An electric pulse emitted and an iridescent flash followed. Then all went quiet and still, her chair now empty. He smiled at the images of what appeared to be two women on the screen.

John Lawson took his pen drive and inserted it into her PC. Pressing the right keys, the images were downloaded onto the device and the screen cleared. He then removed and dropped it in his pocket, sighing with relief.

John started up his PC and organised his workload, humming quietly to himself. His first task was to ensure a letter of resignation with Alison's forged signature be left in her drawer, waiting to be found.

About the Authors

Gordon Aindow is based in Preston, Lancashire, not far from Pendle itself. He writes short stories and poems with an emphasis on life, landscape and love, capturing the fascination and poignancy we can find in situations all around us, if we look a little harder.

He belongs to several locally based writing groups – ScRibble, the Creative Network Writers' Group, and Damson Poets, all of which help to keep up the momentum. Some of his short stories have appeared in the Lancashire Post newspaper.

Gordon has also been involved with collaborations at the Harris Museum in Preston between poets and artworks, resulting in public readings, and involved with Lancashire Archive Office in creative writing projects to commemorate local and international events, such as World War One and Victorian Literary Lancashire. He has performed at several spoken word events · such as What's Your Story, Chorley? · achieved success in local, national and international poetry and short story competitions.

Ruby Red aims to tease, loves to please. She writes fiction and poetry more often combing erotica with vampirism. She has featured in *Coming Together in Verse* published by Smashwords, and her own story collections *Dark*

Secret and *The Dark Night* are available on *museithuppublishing.com*

Darren Melia hails from Liverpool and enjoys writing poetry and short stories, mainly just for his own entertainment. He enjoys factual history but has a particular interest in old folk tales and the supernatural.

His poem in this collection took about 10 minutes to write and comes from the point of view of one of the 'witches' children whose spirt lives on in a later descendant. He describes it as "about the injustice and how that injustice lives on and breeds resentment and a need for some sort of revenge."

Jason D. Brawn was born on the exact date as the original Texas Chainsaw Massacre, and was raised in Alfred Hitchcock's childhood town. After graduating with a BA in Film and Media at Birkbeck College, University of London, Jason decided that creative writing was his forte.

His short fiction and poetry have been featured in a plethora of anthologies, magazines and webzines, and he has also written for the stage, radio, film and comic books.

Jason resides in London and enjoys reading, cinema, theatre, art, cooking, travelling, and listening to obscure music.

Joan Salter was born in Widnes when it was still part of Lancashire, in 1930. She spent the war dodging Luftwaffe bombs, having escaped the Blackpool boarding house to which had been originally evacuated. She wrote *A Game of Cards* aged 16 and it has finally seen print some 70 years later. By a strange turn of fate, she now lives in Blackpool.

Kevin Patrick McCann has published seven collections of poems for adults and one for children, *Diary of a Shapeshifter* (Beul Aithris), a book of ghost stories, *It's Gone Dark* (FeedAread.com Publishing) and *Teach Yourself Self-Publishing* (Hodder) co-written with the playwright Tom Green. He is currently working on his selected poems (his previous collections are out of print) and recently revised a new edition of the ghost stories.

He now publishes under the name of Kevin Patrick McCann to avoid further confusion between himself and other Kevin McCanns currently roaming cyberspace. His Facebook feed is @Diary of a Shapeshifter.

Norbert Gora is a poet and writer from Poland. He is an author of more than 100 poems, which have been published in poetry anthologies around the world - in United States of America, UK, India, Nigeria, Kenya and Australia. In his writing can be seen the mix of the light emotions, full of happiness and dark, "horrorful" experiences of life.

Chris Newton is the singer and lyricist of the Blackpool-based punk band Dischord, renowned in the UK scene for their elaborate albums and energetic live performances. Their latest album *War Or Peace* was described by Musically Fresh as "beautifully crafted and lyrically untouchable".

His writing credits include the black comedy novels *Life Begins at 40* and its sequel *Behind the Sofa*, co-written with Mark Charlesworth. His ghost story 'Grim' was featured in the 2017 *Crowvus Christmas Spirit* anthology.

Chris has been obsessed by witches, ghosts and all things supernatural ever since he was a boy. When people ask him why, he replies "I'm from Witch County."

Chrissy Derbyshire is a writer, storyteller and folklorist, and has previously contributed to the Honno anthology *The Wish Dog and Other Stories: Haunting Tales from Welsh Women Writers* and the History Press anthology *Ballad Tales: An Anthology of British Ballads Retold,* as well as having her own collection of poetry and short stories, *Mysteries*, published by Awen Publications.

Shannon Fries currently lives in Duluth, MN USA, where sweeping cliffs, rock faces, and a lake so large the locals call it "Inner Sea", remind her of her ancestral home in the Highlands of Scotland. She spends her free time hiking the hills with her dogs, writing, and expressing her creativity in any way she can. She dreams of flying the currents above Skye someday.

Juleigh Howard-Hobson is English born with family from Staffordshire, but now lives in the rural Pacific Northwest of the United States, a place of mists and fogs and woods and hills. Her poetry has appeared in *New Witch, Silver Blade, Illumen, Enchanted Conversation, Liquid Imagination, Polu Texni, Abridged Magazine: The Wormwood Issue, Dark Gothic Resurrected Magazine, Illumen, Spirit's Tincture, Faerie Magazine, Rosette Malefcarum, Star*Line, "The Literary Whip"* (Zoetic Press podcast), *The 2018 Rhysling Award Anthology* (Science Fiction Poetry Association), *Weaving the Terrain* (Dos Gatos), *Mandragora* (Scarlett Imprint) and many other places.

She writes of English and European folklore, unseen folk and folkways for the Hadean Black Publishing blog. A Million Writers Award "Notable Story" writer, she has been nominated for the "Best of the Net" and the Pushcart Prize (twice), has been shortlisted for the Morton Marr and the Angels and Devils Poetry Prize (Holland Park Press). She edited the Arêtes Vakreste Boker award winning collection, *Undertow*, was former Assistant Poetry Editor of Able Muse as well as a Predators and Editor's top ten finisher (single poem). Her fifth and most recent formal poetry collection is *Our Otherworld* (Red Salon Press).

Kathleen Halecki possesses a B.A. and M.A. in history, and a doctoral degree in interdisciplinary studies with a focus on early modern Scotland. Although born in New York, she currently resides in a seventeenth century home in New England. Her work can be found in *The Copperfield Review, Shadows in Salem: Wicked Tales from the Witch City*, and *One Night in Salem*.

Phil Howard is a practicing poet and would like to see poetry restored as an art form, appreciated by all through relevant and accessible work that tackles compelling subject matter. Some of his newer poetry has been published in various anthologies such as *The Stony Thursday Book, Crossings Over: Poetry from the Cheshire Prize for Literature 2016* and *Inspired by my Museum*. His poems have also featured on websites such as The Health of the North and The Film Mag, on a Park Trail in Yorkshire and in poetry magazines such as Snakeskin, Decanto and Prole. In 2015 he was also involved in performance events held at Preston's Harris Museum & Art Gallery which related to two exhibitions: 'Picture the Poet', a travelling exhibition from the

National Portrait Gallery, and 'A Green and Pleasant Land? Rural Life in Art'.

Zowie Swan is one half of the creative lunacy behind *Convent Crescent*, a new British horror novel, and also of the recently released short horror film of the same name, Directed by her co-creator (and co-conspirator) Chris Newton.

She has recently completed her first novel, *Mordecai*, a dark and deranged thriller of one woman's struggle with mental illness, love and the supernatural.

Zowie is also the bassist and backing vocalist of the ferocious and energetic punk band Dischord, renowned in their scene for their fierce social commentary and relentless passion.

She takes her inspiration from Terry Pratchett, Neil Gaiman and Angela Carter.

Adele V Robinson is a Lancaster University graduate and a founder member of Lancashire Dead Good Poets' Society. She edited the poetry collection *Walking on Wyre* (available from Amazon), and is Wyre Poet in Residence. Her poem '... from me to you', has been carved onto a memorial to organ donors at Victoria Hospital, Blackpool.

Bridget Kenny is from the South East of Ireland. For as far back as she can remember, Bridget has been keen interested in the paranormal and mediumship, particularly in trying to proof its existence. She also has a huge interest in myths, legends and stories of mythical creatures.

Barra Bromley first came to writing by way of a Post Graduate Diploma in Photojournalism. She believes both arts are equal in creating visual narratives and especially loves photographing the quirky, while turning her writing to the supernatural and horror. Her story in this particular publication explores how our greatest fears often come from within. When she isn't writing strange tales from her base in London, she is taking what are hopefully even stranger photographs. Find her on Twitter: @BarraBromley

Petula Mitchell has always been a keen writer and more recently decided to branch into publication of her work. Her first accepted piece with Frith Books, an English indie publisher, is a stand-alone e-book to be included in an anthology later in 2018, along with a story for another Spooky Isles anthology. When not writing, Petula works at a Doctors surgery as a phlebotomist and nursing assistant.

Alicia Cole is a writer and artist in Huntsville, AL. She is the editor of Priestess & Hierophant Press, the Interviews Editor of *Black Fox Literary Magazine*, the Smashwords Manager of *Femspec Journal*, intern for *256 Magazine* and also writes for *Funky Feminist*. Her work has recently appeared in *TAB: A Journal of Poetry and Poetics*, *Atlas & Alice*, *and Man in the Street Magazine*, and is forthcoming in *Cascadia Subduction Zone*, *Split Lip Magazine*, and *Witches & Pagans*. She loves coffee, plants, animals, and art.

Janet Kenny is a prize winning poet and short story writer based in Blackpool, Lancashire. Her stories have been featured in the Lancashire Post, and her poetry featured in the anthology *Gem* published by Capricorn

Writers, being a winner in the Liz Huf Memorial Literature Awards. She has performed her work at Lancashire Dead Good Poets and more recently has taken up sketch writing for radio and stage performers.

Barry McCann is an award winning writer, editor, broadcaster and speaker. He has written articles for various magazines including Scream, newspapers and websites such as Cultbox and Spooky Isles, and has made regular appearances on BBC Radio Lancashire as resident writer, Radio Cumbria as Folklore Correspondent/ storyteller and Radio Merseyside as cultural historian.

His short stories are regularly featured in the Lancashire Post, American anthologies such *as Dark Gothic Resurrected* and *The Horror Zine*, and the Dracula Society anthology *His Red Eyes Again* (available from Amazon), as well as performing them to audiences across the U.K. and Ireland. In 2012 he received an Ingrid Pitt Queen of Horror award for his short story, *Angel Shall Gather*. It was presented to him by James Herbert.

Barry is also editor of the art and literature journal *Parnassus* for Mensa International, and more recently become a scriptwriter for The Trudy Lite Show currently broadcasting on Amazon Prime.

Lightning Source UK Ltd.
Milton Keynes UK
UKHW012007251119
354217UK00002B/167/P

9 781916 422711